"Aren't I just a bit more handsome now?"

She ignored the question, convinced she could never tell him how his face drew her in, how each eye creased when he smiled, or how his strength flowed from his muscular stature right through her when his arm pulled her close. If she breathed one of these sentiments, she might lean closer and kiss him. Right here. Right in front of God and everybody. "Oh, you were such a brat, teasing us girls and all."

"*I* was, was I? If I remember right, you and your sister, Dot, were quite the instigators when it came to trouble. You'd raise havoc and blame it on me, knowing my mother would always believe sweet, innocent girls. But I couldn't keep my eyes off you. I think at fifteen years old, I was already madly in love." He tugged her to him and tickled her sides as he had when they were younger.

As suddenly as he started, he stopped, jerked his hands back, and sobered. Abby couldn't tell who was the most startled. He cleared his throat. "I'm sorry. I had no right to behave so. Please forgive me, Abby."

They both quieted, not a sound except the loud beating ears.

LINDA S. GLAZ

is an agent with Hartline Literary Agency. Over the years she has served as a meteorologist in the Air Force, has taught karate and women's self-defense, and refereed soccer. She now works part-time in a physical therapy clinic, which is convenient after all the soccer/karate injuries she's sustained.

She relaxes by attending as much theater as her wallet allows, and loves to hunt for props and costumes for local productions.

Linda has a terrific husband, three fabulous kids and three amazing grandchildren. Can life get any better than this?

LINDA S. GLAZ

Always, Abby

HEARTSONG
PRESENTS

Recycling programs
for this product may
not exist in your area.

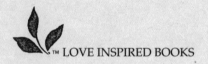 ™ LOVE INSPIRED BOOKS

ISBN-13: 978-0-373-48657-1

ALWAYS, ABBY

Copyright © 2013 by Linda S. Glaz

www.LoveInspiredBooks.com

Printed in U.S.A.

And whoever welcomes one such child in my name welcomes me.
—*Matthew* 18:5

To my wonderful critique partners: Camille Eide, Jessica Nelson, Karla Akins, Cheryl Martin and Emily Hendrickson, who have been true and faithful writing partners in this crazy profession.

Chapter 1

Dachau, April 30, 1945

Will Judge nodded, struggling past the hopeful expressions along the path. After a few minutes of staring into faces filled with fear and relief, he twisted free of the sea of bodies. The smell of decay rushed up, wobbling his steps. He swallowed again and again, but he couldn't stop the rising sadness that filled his throat with bile. Dashing behind a jeep, he leaned against the fender and threw up. Then he wiped his mouth on the back of his sleeve. He sucked back air, needing a deep breath to quell the nerves, but his lungs seized; his stomach lurched again. A quick glance behind brought little comfort. What was taking them so long?

He slouched in the dirt and pulled a letter from his pocket, dizzying a black fly with a swat of the paper. Long braids and a silly grin filled his head. That freckle-faced kid Abigail Richardson had written to him faithfully since he'd left for Germany. Funny girl. What was she now, fifteen or sixteen? Maybe older. He couldn't say. He read the lighthearted story she'd scribbled across the pages and it brought a smile; no doubt her thoughtful intent. Years past, when her family was stranded at the Judges' home for Christmas, he had terrorized her, bullied her, made her giggle and cry. She was a skinny little mouse back then.

That was a long time ago, a long way from here.

He folded the letter and put it in his pocket next to the cologne-soaked love letter from Jeannine. A sigh escaped his lips. Now there was a woman! All the curves and attitude one man could hope for. Although they'd only had a couple of dates, her letters filled his heart with talk of a sweet life together once he returned. A sigh of hope caused his fingers to tingle and tremble as he patted his pocket. He could almost hear his mother, finger pointed, lips pursed: "And what do you know about the girl other than she has a beautiful face and curves?"

His mother would be right, of course, but he and Jeannine had come to know each other quite well from the steady flow of letters. All their hopes and dreams filled each page, giving him a reason to get back home alive.

The fly buzzed him again, this time with reinforcements, pulling his mind back to the present. The odor of sewage slithered into his nostrils and assaulted his senses. He walked around the vehicle and stared. Putting on a good face, he waved his hand as he marched closer.

Withered remnants of humanity cheered, tossed tattered hats in the air and supported themselves as best they could on scraps of wood or the barbed wire fencing. Souls waiting to be filled with something—anything but the lingering fear of the Third Reich.

A pale arm in faded striped clothing reached through the fence as if functioning on its own and clutched Will's hand with bony fingers. Then another and another until Will staggered against outstretched limbs. They seemed to hang on in case he'd change his mind about their liberation and leave them, once again, to the Nazis.

"American? Yank, yes?" Another man grabbed while two others dropped to their knees in the dirt to pray and dozens of others simply fell over, the excitement almost too much exertion.

Will swallowed hard. He couldn't wait another second for these gates to be opened wide. Nor should he. The people had a right to be freed. He rose up with a determination in his bones he hadn't felt before and ripped wire clippers from a back pouch. Marching around the vehicle, back to the barbed-wire fence, he cut through one line at a time until an entire section had been removed.

As the fence separated, a collective cheer bathed in tears rose to the heavens, and hundreds of voices started singing. What song? He wasn't sure. In Will's mind his own favorite, "Amazing Grace," churned like notes through a bagpipe. And he whistled the tune.

With the fence at his feet he expected a rush to freedom, but as suddenly as the cheers had erupted, an eerie quiet settled over the camp. No one moved. Only questioning looks: first to him, then to the fence and finally to each other. Again, not a soul put a foot forward. What was wrong?

Though the gaping mouth of liberation awaited, the men and women remained inside the camp. Why didn't they leave? Were they afraid this was a trick? They must think the Americans were really Nazis playing another hateful game with them. Will had heard horrific stories of how the soldiers had toyed with their captives.

He shuffled dust up with his feet as he motioned for them to move away from the confines of the camp. "Come out." He swung his arms in large arcs, sending the dust clouds in all directions. "You're free. Come on. What's wrong?" The prisoners seemed to be holding a singular breath. No one moved.

For the longest time Will remained rooted in place, unsure what to say or do next. Surely one brave soul would break through the fence and bask in the freedom. He tugged at his collar, heat seeping up his neck.

No one budged from the nightmare but a small boy.

Only about three years old by Will's account. It was hard to tell, what with the wide eyes sunken into such a hollow face. The tiny creature, also dressed in striped pajama-style clothing, inched forward, looked about, took a few more steps and then wrapped his arms around Will's leg. Hanging on *oh so* tight, he smiled through tears until he'd bathed the leg of Will's uniform like an overturned baptismal fount. Abigail Richardson came to mind again, but even skinny tomboy Abby hadn't looked like this. The boy was nothing but skin and bony protrusions. And a huge smile. Cold fingers clung to Will's thigh, digging in for dear life.

Will rubbed the boy's head. "You got folks here, fella? You're one brave little man."

Silent, but with a determined look, the boy glanced up, held out his open hand. "Take, Yank." His skinny fingers revealed a dried-out crust of bread, sticky with sweat and dirt, no doubt misered away from his last meal, and now offered as a thank-you. Instant realization of the magnitude of the gift moved Will's heart. The widow's mite—from a child. He bent down, fighting tears of his own, and tugged the boy to his chest.

May 12, 1945

Abigail Richardson finished diapering her sweet niece and swaddled her into a soft flannel receiving blanket. Such a precious bundle. She could hardly wait for the day when she would have babies of her own, not be merely Aunt Abby, as she was now.

Her sister Barbara opened her arms and accepted the squirming infant. "Oh, Abby, isn't she a joy? Have you ever seen such a beautiful and content baby? Who would have thought three years ago when I left home to come be part of Betty's wedding, I'd marry that handsome brother of hers and we would have such a beautiful baby girl." Barbara's gaze listed across the room and fell on Jackson Judge.

Abby reached out, palming the peaches-and-cream cheeks. She had babysat a multitude of neighbor children, but none so lovely as Grace. "With these gorgeous eyes, she's her daddy's girl, you know."

Jackson stood halfway across the room acting as if he were afraid touching the infant might break her. But he had a lopsided grin on his face that Abby would have sworn said, *look what I did.*

She hoped one day to have a loving marriage like her sister Barbara and her brother-in-law, Jackson. Theirs was a fairytale love story. They were meant to be together in spite of the Pearl Harbor tragedy that had tried to keep them apart.

Once Jackson had come out of his shell after being so badly burned, and realized that Barbara loved him scars and all, he'd married her almost immediately. And now here was Abby helping her sister. And what a blessing the birth of Grace Marie had been just four days earlier, the same day Germany had finally surrendered.

A wonderful time for new life to start.

Abby sighed. Her own new start didn't involve babies, but the trip here *had* offered her hope. And she needed a second chance after the way she had let her parents down recently.

She met Jackson's eyes and blushed. His brother Will looked older now, too, judging from his photo. She'd written him sporadically since they first met, but weekly since he'd gone overseas. He must be quite a prize. The army didn't accept chubby little boys, did they? No, from the one photo she'd seen in the Judges' home, he was tall and filled out now. After all, he was twenty years old, if she remembered right. At fifteen he'd been a pudgy, lackluster monster whose entire goal in life had been to tease her to tears. But as she'd come to understand, monsters can grow into handsome men given half a chance.

Turning on her heel, she motioned to Jackson. "You'd better come sit with your wife. She's not the type to raise this little punkin all by herself, you know. I understand she has very specific ideas about a daddy's role in bringing up the baby."

He cocked a grin. "You don't need to remind me. If anyone realizes how headstrong my beautiful wife is, I do." He winked at mother and daughter and Abby eased from the room to allow them some privacy. There were things they no doubt wanted to say, words that mustn't be murmured within earshot of others.

As Abby tiptoed out, little Grace started a squall that could be heard all the way to Mayor Judge's peanut factory. The baby already showed signs of being stubborn when she wanted her own way, and in a mere four days had managed to wrap her parents around her tiny pink fingers.

In the hallway Abby's eyes filled as she recalled the Christmas when the Judges had pulled them from a flood into a warm and inviting home. This family from New Hope, Tennessee, had taken the Richardsons in and saved not only their Christmas, but their lives. And nearly five years later the two families had combined into one through baby Grace. Abby let out a huge sigh as she made her way to the front of the house. She gazed out the window, looking up and down the street. Spring flowers bloomed in front of each home where she knew love tended the gardens. But her interest wasn't in the flowers. Now she was anxious for the mailman to see if any word would come from Will.

Her heart did a foolish gallop that brought her to her senses. She smoothed her skirt and shook her head. Not that she cared about a silly old letter. Of course not. But it might put Mrs. Judge's mind to rest knowing her son was safe. So she continued to watch for the mailman—for Mrs. Judge.

Abby spun from the window. Who was she kidding? She hadn't seen that boy of theirs since the year of their rescue when he'd stood on the porch, mouth filled with peanuts, waving and chomping. After that he'd tied himself to Abby's and Dot's sides, pestering them to no end for the entire time they'd stayed in New Hope. But when Abby had arrived a week ago, almost five years later, and seen his picture on the mantel, she'd stopped and stared. Her jaw had nearly unhinged. He was no longer little Willie Judge at the other end of those pen pal letters. Instead a tall handsome army corporal grinned a smug lemme-at-those-Nazis smile. Plenty of girls in town had no doubt seen that same expression. All Abby could think was peanuts had done wonders for that body.

Heat covered her cheeks again as she recalled her mother's admonitions, and she tamped down the unladylike sentiments. What was wrong with her lately? Was she turning into one of those boy-crazy girls? Her actions of late seemed to imply she lacked a decent upbringing, and anyone who knew Mary Richardson's childrearing tactics realized that was not the case. As Mother said, a girl had to be held accountable for her reputation; no one else could do it for her. It's just that young Will had been so adorable when he'd pulled her hair, tweaked her nose and taunted her. At least that was how she remembered him.

Now he looked like he'd be a different kind of threat; one that might tease her heart, instead, and leave her breathless. She choked on the romantic notions crossing her mind once again. *Get control of yourself, Abi-*

gail. Stop this nonsense pining over a boy who probably doesn't even care you're alive.

Maybe an ice-cold glass of milk was in store. Humming a lullaby, Abby padded toward the kitchen where she knew there would be cookies to go with the milk. But halfway there, she stopped and listened.

At the sound of sniffling, her feet carried her, instead, into the parlor where Mrs. Judge sat with her face to the window, a paper in her hands. Maybe she'd rather be left alone. Another sniffle. "Abigail, dear, is that you?"

And maybe not. Abby strolled forward, touched the slumped shoulder. "Is everything all right, Mrs. Judge? Did the mailman get here already?" The woman must have received bad news. That meant only one thing. Will. A rat-a-tat filled her chest as her heart beat faster than usual. She licked her lips, not wanting to ask, but unable to stop herself from blurting out, "Is there...anything I can get you?" Cookies and milk weren't going to heal a mother's heart if there was unsettling news about Will.

Mrs. Judge turned, eyes rimmed in red. "Oh, Abigail. I'm glad you're here, dear. So happy your folks let you come to visit." Her fingers crushed the sheet of paper. "What would we have done without you, child?"

What, indeed. She only hoped she hadn't been in the way when Barbara had gone into labor. It had all happened so fast, Jackson hadn't taken the time to get Barbara to the hospital or even call the doctor from the clinic in town. Now Mrs. Judge, a normally robust woman with the energy of a dozen firecrackers, sat alone tugging at a scrap of paper. Abigail felt she shouldn't ask. No news was good news, right? If she didn't put her thoughts into words, everything would be fine.

She sighed at her foolishness and eased onto the sofa next to Mrs. Judge. "Is your letter…from Will?" *Oh, please say you haven't received bad news about Will. Not Will.*

The woman's forehead creased. She drew in a deep breath before she spoke. "Not a letter, dear." Withdrawing a hankie from her sleeve, she dabbed at her eyes. Then, as though the floodgates of her heart had opened, she turned to Abby and cried, "A telegram. William is missing."

Will smiled at Hank's short legs struggling to keep up at his side. Feeling more out of place in Poland that in Germany, Will kept vigilant, unsure what to expect. Hank trembled with each step.

Perhaps if his health were better. But the Nazis had seen to that. He recalled the looks on the Germans' faces after the exhausting tour where the last German citizen from the outlying area had stepped through the opening in the barbed wire. Like it or not, the Americans had forced the neighboring people to see what remained of Dachau.

Sentiments ran deeper than the Americans could have imagined. Some believable, others not so much. Were these people victims as well or were they conspirators with the Nazis? Even the guilty hid behind masks of concern, no one the wiser.

"Ve did not know."

"How could dey do dis?"

"You tink ve allow dis? Ve do not know what go on here."

A refined and obviously well-educated woman grabbed Will's hands. "We did not realize. You must believe me when I say this." Tears flowed down her cheeks as her husband led her away, both mumbling their innocence as they hurried from the empty camp.

Will couldn't tell one way or the other whether they did or didn't know what had transpired at Dachau, though he certainly had his opinion. But it mattered not. The camp's atrocities were over and done. Whether or not the community understood, simply stood by or had no inkling didn't figure into the scheme of things anymore. The Americans had marched in, taken control, and now the Nazis had better run if they knew what was good for them.

He had stared long at the woman's back, wondering whether the tears had been real or she'd merely been doing her best to escape the rage of a very angry world.

With a shake of his head Will took in the round eyes again; eyes that stared at him, hands that tugged at his pant legs. Will longed to have five minutes alone with whoever was responsible for the emaciated little boy at his side. Just five minutes; that's all he would need to put things to right.

In all their questioning no one had known who the child belonged to. A woman told him in broken English the boy was Polish, not German, and that his parents were dead. "He has no one here now. His name is Henryk Drobinski."

Will squeezed the scrawny shoulder. He didn't look like a Henryk. Those big brown eyes appeared far too vulnerable for an oversize name like Drobinski. Too small and malnourished, he was a four-year-old orphan, another casualty of Hitler's insanity gone unchecked.

Now here they were looking for relatives; Was it a fool's errand?

Nearly two weeks after Dachau's emancipation, hiking near the Polish border after the short train ride, Will slowed enough for Hank to keep up. Unsure exactly *where* that put them. How had things gotten so mixed up since the day Will was assured they would locate Hank's kin?

That had been the first week of May. As the huge trucks pulled away from the camp, loaded with men and women anxious to return and find out what had happened to their homes, Hank had continued his vigil alongside Will. A woman, withered from months of internment, reached out a shrunken hand from the last truck, gesturing at the boy to join them, but he refused to leave his Yank "Vill."

When one of the troops tried to pry the scrawny fingers from Will's leg, the man laughed at Hank's persistence, threw his hands in the air, and declared, "That little fella's stuck like a tick on ol' Blue. I guess you have a kid, now, Will." Will gazed down at his tick and shrugged. "I guess I do, Eddie. I guess I do at that."

"You gonna stay hooked to me, Hank?" Will knew the answer before he finished the question. What would the boy do on his own? He had found a willing sap to cling to.

The boy let go for a brief second and pointed Will's direction. "I Hank."

"*You're* Hank. I'm Will." He indicated the pitiful

sunken chest then his own as he'd done dozens of times with no reaction. Maybe if he…

"I Hank?"

Yes! "That's right. You're Hank. Henryk's too big a name for a little guy like you. From now on, you're Hank."

As his thumb jammed into his chest, a huge smile splayed across Hank's face. "I Hank. You Yank." He giggled at his joke, then stopped just as quickly to paw through Will's pack in case he'd missed a crumb earlier. "More? You got more?"

One thing was sure, Hank ate like a half-starved soldier. Where did the little guy put it all? Will snatched a piece of gum from his back pocket and motioned for Hank to chew, not swallow.

That day had completely changed his life. He'd looked up when Sgt. McGuffey had joined them. His face, long and subdued, boding no good.

"Willie, boy. The kid's folks are gone. They were killed a couple of weeks ago when the Nazis figured we were days away. Killed so many people, they couldn't bury them all. We found who we're told were his folks in a big open pit out back. An old Polish woman who knew the family. She was cryin' like a baby when she gave us the names of about a dozen of the people who were shot just days before. Dumped into the open grave. Half filled in, half not. Probably ran out of warm bodies to do the digging for them. The only prisoners left didn't have the energy to move from building to building let alone close graves."

Did Hank know his parents lay just behind the buildings? Had he been present when the Nazis had put rifles to their heads and marched them away?

"What'll happen to Hank? He doesn't have aunts or uncles here. No relatives at all that anyone knows about." Will couldn't allow the boy to be taken to an orphanage. "I'm not about to have the very people who saw the smoke, heard the screams and still pretended not to know about Dachau take care of him." In reality he appreciated the fact there must have been, must *be* plenty of good people living near who were as shocked as the rest of the world, but Will wasn't willing to search them out, wasn't willing to take the chance.

The sergeant slapped a stick against his palm, the thump-thumping breaking the spell. "There aren't a whole lot of choices, here, soldier. I'm sure they'll have programs up and running in no time to find homes for these kids." He leaned in and spoke in a low voice. "At least the Polish kids. Ones who aren't, you know, Jewish. And Hank oughtta do fine. Some nice German family."

"Stop. Nice German family? Maybe one of the hundreds who closed their eyes or looked the other way when Hank, here, was being systematically starved to death? That sound like a nice home to you? I won't hear of it. I absolutely have to find some of his relatives for him to stay with." Will patted the overstuffed backpack on his arm. "Shouldn't take too long, just across the border."

Thump-thump. "It's your hide if the higher-ups find out what you're doing. Think of yourself, Willie boy. We're about to head home. Think of yourself for once."

He *was* thinking of himself, and how he would never be able to live with himself if he didn't locate Hank's relatives. This war had caused many a hard heart, but his wouldn't be one of them. He still had to look out for the underdogs.

First Will's commander had offered to allow him to escort the boy to a small town west of the Odra River, the place he was rumored to have come from. But since there was no way to prove the boy was Polish other than his name and the word of that woman, it was decided Will would take him to the border and see if there had been any inquiries. Two days later as trucks began to roll, another officer withdrew permission and ordered him to muster with his unit.

Dear God. How can I leave without finding him a home? Please, make the impossible possible.

Then an hour later as the men packed their gear and Hank stood by watching Will's every move, the commander sought him out, clapped him on the back and placed two train tickets in his hand. He told Will to hurry and leave before anyone noticed. "Here are orders for when you return. Hurry or we'll all be gone." He shook his head. "Good luck, m'boy."

Will hadn't a clue whether he'd been granted permission or if the commander had merely looked the other way. At any rate this was the opportunity he'd been waiting for.

He remembered the commander's last sobering words before he tucked the orders into his jacket pocket and hoisted Hank onto his shoulders. "Be careful. There are still some stragglers who don't know the war's over."

No doubt a good many who wouldn't surrender no matter what. But his hope never flagged as they set out for Poland.

On the way some folks waved and cheered, others turned their backs, walked along heads down, afraid the Nazis would soon gain control again and start the reign of terror one more time. They didn't dare collaborate with an American. Will understood without a single soul explaining it to him. He saw the fear etched across many faces.

Here, this morning, in the small farming village, the last door had shut in Will and Hank's faces with a finality that spoke of years of fear. The townspeople had told Will to pack up the boy and leave.

"We know nothing. No food here. You go."

Vacant eyes peeked between the crack in a door. "Take boy away. No trouble. We know no one with name of Drobinski."

"You leave, Yank." With arms wide, tears trickling down the man's face, he shook his head sadly. "Please go, I have family to care for. I would like to help, but I cannot."

Well doggone it, that's what Will was hunting for—family. A family who would care for one small boy. He stopped in the middle of town and shouted "Doesn't anyone know the Drobinskis?" He kicked the dirt and lifted Hank into his arms. Hank snuggled in, safe in the Yank's grasp.

After all the walking they'd done, then the dismal train ride to get here, these last acts of cruelty from the frightened Polish people hit Will the hardest. They were back where they had started the first of May.

So Hank and Will retraced their steps until they came to the small village leading to the train tracks. Both exhausted and defeated, they dragged tired feet over the stony path and continued on west.

Hank tugged Will's arm. "Eat?" The boy's favorite word.

"Not yet, buddy. We'll stop when we get to the train station." He hoisted his fist and made a chug-chug gesture. "Train. Woo-woo."

The tiny fist pumped the air. "Woo-woo. Train. Woo-woo."

Chapter 2

Abby tried all week to coax a genuine smile from Mrs. Judge's lips. Oh, she smiled, but with the look of one putting up a good front. Abby knew the difference.

"Maybe some of those sugar cookies with lots of frosting. Jackson said they're your favorites. With pink frosting in honor of your precious granddaughter, Gracie."

"That would be lovely, dear. We can send a plate with all of you when you and Jackson and Barbara take little Grace back to their house tomorrow morning." Her chin trembled as if she wanted to say more, but didn't know what might come out. After a few seconds she mumbled, "If only we knew where he was. How can the army lose a soldier? The telegram said he'd gone to Poland to find a boy's parents or family—something or other. Aren't there organizations or agencies to take care of lost children?" Her eyes clouded. "I'm sorry. That sounded callous, didn't it? I'm sure William is doing what he feels is right. Only, what if—"

Abby reached out and patted Mrs. Judge's arm. "Please don't think that way. I'm sure he's fine." Unsure what to say next to cheer Mrs. Judge, she decided she'd start the cookies. "I'll see about the sugar. If we need more, I'll run to the store. *If* we haven't used up your ration on all of our baking."

Mrs. Judge shook her head. "No, dear. The coupons are in the drawer next to the silverware." She didn't move. Didn't take a deep breath. Mrs. Judge sat on the sofa and stared at the picture of Will on the mantel. Her lips twittered and jittered nonstop. Abby recognized the faithful prayers of a mother's heart.

She dashed to the kitchen, her gardening slacks rustling with each step. There she leaned against the counter. Will's mix-up must be in the paperwork. Of course. Those things happened all the time. Any minute now Mrs. Judge would receive a telegram explaining the foul-up. Abby stopped her silly daydreams and compelled herself to concentrate on the here and now. She rummaged through the cupboard and found she needed sugar after all. Grabbing the ration book, she donned a light sweater and scooted out the front door before she could be a party to any more sniffles or wild imaginings. *Or* before Mrs. Judge could remind her to change out of her pants.

Lord, hasn't the Judge family suffered enough with Jackson being injured at Pearl Harbor? Now Will— missing. The army ought to have rules so they could keep track of their men. If her father oversaw the army, there would be plenty of rules, like at home.

Although she didn't remember there being as many when Barbara was growing up. Maybe her father hadn't needed to be as strict with his Bunny. Abby sighed. Life had birthed a litter of problems, her being one of theirs.

Their words echoed through her head. *Abigail, the young man might be a churchgoer, but that doesn't mean he's a believer. You will not go out with him alone.*

But, Dad. I'm eighteen years old. Not a baby. When will you stop treating me like a child?

When you stop acting like one.

It was the only time she remembered talking back to her father. And all because of first love.

Michael Kennison—persuasive and handsome. He'd wanted to marry her but had insisted her parents would never allow them to be together. Was she a woman or a child? After two straight days of arguing, he'd convinced her she only had one choice: run away with him.

Will rushed Hank from the family-run restaurant. Nothing but nasty looks from most of the patrons. He should have worn civilian clothes, but that might have been more dangerous yet. Eyes followed the two from the establishment until they hit the outskirts of the town where they would catch the train. No one else loitered or waited at the station.

Stretching out on the bench, Will motioned for Hank to sit next to him, but the little guy danced, foot to foot. Will remembered that most uncomfortable feeling as a boy. So he gestured around the back of the building where Hank could relieve himself in the trees.

He pulled two letters from his pocket, the one from his love, Jeannine, and the other a letter from Abby—

his sister-in-law's kid sister. First he opened the pink-flowered paper still ripe with cologne, and read Jeannine's message. Jeannine's words never ceased to stir his emotions, but Abby's? Abby's letters filled him with home and family. He put Jeannine's letter away and opened Abby's and began to read:

April 15, 1945

Hey there, Will,

I sure hope Uncle Sam's treating you swell. My father says I have no idea, and know what? He's right. I can't imagine. All I can say is you keep safe, do you hear?

I'm so excited that I might get to go to New Hope and visit Jackson and Bunny this spring. Oops, I mean Barbara. She'd be so upset to know I still think of her as Bunny. Oh well, who cares, right? All I care about is the chance to be there when my niece or nephew is born. And the work I do for my father is easily put aside with his blessing. Mother would love to be the one to go, but Dot has been very sickly this year and I don't think she would travel well. So it's up to me to stand in for the family. My father isn't even traveling much anymore. Now that he has his own company, he sends others out. I must say I miss being on the road with him when he checks out the work sites, but there are also advantages to enjoying the comforts of home.

Sorry, guess I'm a-jabbering away and you couldn't care less.

Wish you were going to be there. If I do get to go, I'd love to see you, know you're safe. You and your family have been such wonderful friends. And then when Jackson and Barbara married, it's almost like we're all family. Even you, Will. I guess that makes us like cousins or something instead of just pen pals.

Well, cuz, guess I should let you get back to saving us from the Germans. Ha-ha.

I'm always at the end of a pen, Will, if you ever need a shoulder.

We all think of you and pray for you.

Always,

Abby

Silly Abby. *So we're cousins now, are we?* He laughed. And he remembered Abby with a great deal of affection. What a cutie she was. A line of freckles across her nose, braids that hung down her back, and gangly legs, but what a crush he'd had. The more he tortured her, the more she came back. Life was carefree then, even with the terrible flooding that year. Flood or no flood, it was home.

What a faithful kid to have written him so often. In the meantime he could picture her dashing between the houses as she waited on the birth of Barbara and Jackson's baby. Shucks, she was just a baby herself. But old enough to keep the letters coming—letters packed with stories from home. The news about his family helped him cling with hope to the time when he'd return. He'd have to thank her one day.

Will had to admit that the thought of Jackson being a father felt right.

He pulled Jeannine's letter out again. A letter that kept him hoping for…well, a gentleman didn't think about such things. Not in the Judge household, not with *his* mother in charge of their upbringing. But he still managed a smile.

Following a quick reread, he slipped the notes into his pocket and leaned back, head lolling against the building. Sun warmed his face, reminding him of the hot Tennessee days. He couldn't wait to play baseball this summer with his buddies from high school. How many would be left? So many had joined the war. Even if only one had died, it would be one too many. But then he thought of freeing Hank from the camp and the hardships were all worth it.

He pictured his mother and father sitting on the porch swing. Did they miss him as much as he missed them? And his home? And his friends?

Always, Abby.

Home. Like Dorothy, all he longed for was to be transported to the house he'd grown up in. He'd go in the center of a tornado if that were the only way to return.

The countryside here didn't speak of the horrors the Nazis had perpetrated on the people. A soft breeze lifted the hairs on his neck in a gentle massage. The quiet did little for his nerves, but eventually exhaustion won out and he closed his eyes to wait for the boy. Scrambling noises to his left. Hank or… His eyes flew open. "Who's there?"

Instantly the barrel of a 9mm Luger in the hands of a German soldier rounded the corner of the building.

And he shoved the weapon into Will's side before he could jump up from the bench. The soldier pressed a finger to his lips, telling Will not to say a word. "Come with me. My prisoner."

Will rose, crossing his hands back and forth. "Hey, buddy. The war's over. Done. No more."

"I tell you when war's over, Yank." He jammed Will harder under the arm with the barrel.

Will eyed the corner of the building. The boy might show up and get hurt. His stabs at persuasion failed; the soldier having none of his rhetoric about the war ending. When Will didn't move, the man lifted the weapon and cracked metal against Will's head. He crumpled back to the seat, supporting a throbbing skull. In seconds sweat speckled his forehead and his hands shook. Just like the commander had said, there were troops who didn't know Germany had surrendered, or who didn't care. One last dead American might be a trophy for this soldier. Will had seen it play out firsthand.

"Gun. Give me gun, *soldat*."

Will pushed down the pain in his head and stood to lift his weapon from the sling over his shoulder. But if he gave the Nazi his rifle, what chance would they have? And there was Hank to think of. He could not let the boy be put in harm's way. His gaze raced over the countryside as if a company of Americans might march in, save the day. No such company arrived. Okay, at this point he'd even settle for a couple of flyboys.

As the German reached for Will's Garand rifle, he lowered his own weapon just a bit, and from nowhere came a thud! A blast to the Nazi's knee from behind.

His face contorted and he twisted around to discover his attacker.

Hank, wielding a piece of pipe almost as big as he was, stood rooted to the ground. He trembled from his hands to his legs, but he held tight to the pipe with a threatening posture—as threatening a posture as a twenty-five-pound nothing could muster. Will leaped around the soldier, grabbed the Garand, and with the butt on the rifle, knocked the man in the head, sending him to the ground.

A train whistle blew an anxious cry in the distance; one that told Will they'd better hustle. He whipped the man's belt off and tied his hands to the bench, then stripped his pants to his ankles and twisted them around his feet in a tight knot. He blew out a long breath and slid the Luger into the back of his pack.

Hank wormed his way into Will's arms. "I good, Vill?"

Will buried his forehead in the child's chest. "You did good, buddy." He whirled toward the soldier. "If you so much as move when that train pulls in, I'll shoot you in the head." He pulled the handgun from his pack again and pointed it toward the man's temple. He'd come through two years of battle and never knowingly killed a man, but he would if he had to in order to protect Hank.

Lt. Karry jabbed Will in the chest. "What do you think he is, some puppy you can hide in your duffel bag and smuggle home?"

"No, sir."

"And where were you, again? We reported you missing a week ago."

Will kept his eyes straight ahead as he addressed the first lieutenant. "Sir, I explained all that. Just ask the commander."

Karry slammed a fist into his palm. "Very convenient, seeing the commander rotated stateside three days ago."

The energy drained from Will's body. "Listen, sir. I'm telling you the truth." The assignment hadn't exactly been sanctioned; now he was sure of that. He might face charges for his little jaunt to the border. If only Commander Barrister had been more specific. But it was what it was and he'd have to accept whatever happened to him.

"Sir, if there's any way you can—"

"Do I look like a charity worker?" Karry stepped toe-to-toe with Will.

Will's arms opened wide. He longed to show the magnitude of his connection to the boy. "He saved my life. Four years old and he took on a lousy soldier to save me." His hand rubbed the stubble on Hank's head. As he looked down, the brown eyes locked onto his and Will smiled, but quickly recovered and straightened his bearing.

The lieutenant sucked air through his teeth. "I'll see what I can do." His glance trailed to Will's knee where the boy had positioned himself once again.

Will's legs turned to rubber thinking of what might happen to Hank if he couldn't go back to the States with him.

Karry retreated a few paces, and Will noticed he couldn't take his eyes off the boy. The lieutenant, like all other troops, understood respecting a soldier, and Hank was a proven soldier after his skirmish with the Nazi.

The lieutenant's face softened. "He'll need medical clearance first before the higher-ups will even consider this request. *If* I'm able to get permission. Don't get your hopes up. Got me, Judge?"

"Yes, sir. I mean, no, sir. I won't, sir."

"You're dismissed." He offered a casual salute to the boy. "And so's Hank."

The boyish grin turned from the lieutenant to Will and back to the lieutenant. "Gonna eat?" He let go of Will's leg and stepped toward Lt. Karry. "Please?"

"Get him outta here. And find some decent clothes for him to wear. He can't stay in that T-shirt of yours forever. Looks like he's wearing a dress for crying out loud." A hint of a smile escaped him, but was immediately replaced with his stoic military demeanor. "And give him a bath. You both stink!"

Abby awoke to the sound of Grace cooing and gurgling. So Barbara could get her first full night's sleep, Jackson had rolled the bassinet into Abby's room, per her request. She did the one o'clock and the four o'clock by glass bottles. But now Grace wanted Mommy and Mommy probably needed Grace.

Changing the baby and wrapping her in the flannel receiving blanket, Abby padded toward Jackson and Barbara's room. They were obviously happy to be back in their own house. Jackson's sister, Betty, and her husband, Ted, were due in from Nashville and would be next door soon. Betty had missed Gracie's birth because she'd been in Nashville with Ted, helping Mrs. Barrymore care for Ted's father. The man had had a heart attack when his oldest son, Teo, had gotten into trouble with the law—and a girl.

Had Michael Kennison been another Teo in the making? She was grateful she'd never have to find out the full extent of his perfidy, though what she did find out was bad enough.

Well Abby wouldn't dwell on that right now. She had this cherished baby to care for. "Here comes Mommy's precious girl," Abby called from the hallway as she rapped on the door.

When she entered the bedroom, she couldn't help notice Jackson was already out. "Everything all right? Is little punkin's daddy at work this early?"

Darkness fell over Barbara's face. "His father called him. There's news about Will at the house. I only hope it isn't…well. We need good news. Please say a prayer, Abigail. I don't know what Mother Judge would do if anything happened to *her* baby."

Abby handed Grace to her sister. "Here. Can you manage on your own?" Not sure why she'd asked such a foolish question, she snuggled Grace into Barbara's eager arms.

"Of course, silly. Why?"

"I'll go to the main house, too, and be with Mrs. Judge. She'll want a woman with her if the word is bad."

Chapter 3

Will spat on his hand and pressed down the newly sprouting hair on Hank's head. "Okay, now, buddy. Let's say it again." He pointed to Hank's chest. "My name is Henryk."

Hank's small finger tapped his chest and he shouted as loud as he could over the clacking of the train. "My name…Hank! Good?"

Will had to laugh. He'd created the monster, now he'd have to live with it. When he'd written that he had a surprise for all his family, he wasn't kidding. And what would Jeannine say about him bringing the boy home? While he figured his parents or Jack and Barbara might have to be the official guardians, he had every intention of being Hank's father. In fact, he couldn't imagine life anymore without the little fella. In only a few short weeks, the boy had wriggled into corners of Will's heart he hadn't even known existed.

He nudged Hank, though he didn't need to ask. "Hungry?"

Hank rubbed his belly—what there was of it—making yummy noises. "Mmm...ungry. Hankungry."

Will threw his head back and laughed. Hank was always hungry. No doubt making up for the time in the concentration camp where Hank had told him he'd eaten barely more than a slice of bread and some weak broth each day.

The military, once the arrangements had been made for Hank to accompany Will home, had put the boy through the works, and the doctors were pleasantly surprised at his overall good health. No TB, no lice, just badly malnourished and dehydrated, but he was catching up pretty fast with Will shoveling in food and milk. At least four pounds in the past two weeks. Maybe more from rehydration than actual weight gain. But Will couldn't be sure the way Hank gobbled man-size meals.

Will reached into his pocket. He'd purchased some candy and tucked the bars inside his jacket after the unscheduled lunch stop for train repairs. "You've been a good boy, Hank." Just a smile at first from Hank. "So I thought maybe a chocolate bar would be in order."

Then the words flowed. "Choclit! *Dziekuje.*" He understood *chocolate* with no difficulty and always managed a heartfelt thank-you without being reminded.

"Here you go." Will pulled the wrapper off, keeping on enough to prevent sticky fingers that would transfer chocolate immediately to the new clothes. "We'll be in New Hope in an hour."

Hank's eyes grew round and sparkled as he chomped off a big chunk. "Hope?"

"Yeah, buddy. For you, it's going to mean hope." *For me? Not so sure.* There they would face his family, including a new niece. And, of course, Jeannine.

Abby comforted Grace while Barbara adjusted her stylish new hat so it wouldn't blow away. The Judge family waited on the platform. After an hour they were informed the train had been detained along the route— a two-hour delay.

Mr. Judge spoke up over complaints. "I could drive everyone home for the two hours, or we can stay here, have a soda and wait for Will."

Barbara decided to return home because of Grace, and Abby offered to accompany her. But Jackson scooped mother and daughter into his arm. "I'll take them, Abby. You wait for the train with Mother and Father. And don't smudge that pretty yellow blouse. You look so lovely."

Mrs. Judge alternated between laughing and crying, anticipating her son's return. "I feel so foolish, now don't I? One minute I imagine all the bad things that might have happened and the next I'm so grateful they found him and he's coming home. Isn't that silly?" She primped her hair for what must have been the tenth time, the humidity causing a lazy droop to her curls. "After that telegram, why, I thought we'd lost him for sure. Now, it seems so foolish I worried like I did."

Mr. Judge drew closer and wrapped his arms around his wife. "Not foolish at all. You're his mama. You're entitled. Why, he won't even recognize our Abigail here, will he?" He tendered a smile Abby's direction, his glistening eyes giving away the fact he was every bit as excited to have Will home as his wife. "You haven't seen William since you were what, thirteen? Fourteen? That's right, isn't it? You didn't get to come to Barbara and Jackson's wedding. Chicken pox, I believe."

"I so wish I'd been here. I had to stay with my aunt. I haven't seen Will since the flood nearly five years ago."

"Seems to me he was always yanking on your hair or tweaking your nose, something like that." Mr. Judge's eyes sparkled. "He's all boy, our Will."

Probably just like his father.

"And don't forget the pine branches under your covers. My, but I'll bet they were prickly."

Abby blushed. She recalled with no effort. Then after Christmas, when the Richardson family had climbed into their car to go home after the flood, Will reached through the window and pulled her braid one last time. "Write me now and then," he'd said. Her heart flipped in her chest just remembering.

"It's been a long time, Mr. Judge. I don't s'pose I'd recognize him either except for the pictures on the mantel. You're right. I was fourteen and he was fifteen. I can remember a teenager shoving peanuts into his mouth. I'll bet he's much taller now." And broader, and filled out from training, and, oh, why did she have to think about him like this? Other than their friendly letters, he no doubt hadn't given her one thought in years.

Abby released a long sigh. "Why doesn't that train hurry?"

Mrs. Judge glanced her way, a smile spread across her face.

Abby swallowed hard but was sure a blush covered her cheeks.

Before long the familiar whistle accompanied a whoosh of steam and a great deal of noise. Screeching brakes brought the monster to a stop. Heads bobbed in all directions as people strained to see their loved ones exit.

Folks piled out of the compartments in streams. Soldiers returning home, aunts, uncles, grandparents arriving for reunions. Families waited on the platform along with bags and trunks. More people than Abby had expected. But not the one she longed to see. Not yet.

Then, through a puff of vapor, she spotted him—William Judge. Nothing like she remembered. He was taller, all right, and dignified. Handsome as all get-out. Oh. She could have picked him from any crowd. A person's eyes didn't change with time. They either glimmered with life, or they didn't. Will's did. Then his smile swooped over the family in a huge crush of recognition. Was he smiling at her? Amazing that he remembered her after all these years. But he definitely stared right in her direction. Imagine, after all this time, he'd still be interested in her. She clamped a hand over her mouth to stifle a giggle.

Her heart beat a steady rhythm, louder and louder, as he strode straight toward her holding out long, muscled arms. She wanted to cry and rush into them. Tell him the letters had meant as much to her as to him. If truth be told, she had fallen in love with him through the stories and she longed to know if he felt the same. He must. After all, he'd written each week confiding his most personal thoughts. While her heart beat a rapid drumroll in her chest, she bit the edge of her lip, waiting. Did he expect her to run into his arms? She closed her eyes briefly, wondering what she should do. Then she opened them to welcome him. Her excitement prevented her from calling out his name, but surely her face must give away her most intimate feelings.

All their shared words flooded her thoughts in a matter of seconds. *Love ya, kiddo. You make me miss home. I'll bet you're all grown up now, not that silly little tomboy anymore.* Could he read her mind?

One step more and he would be…

…beyond her.

"Jeannine. Honey." A beautiful redhead rushed boldly off the platform from behind them and down the steps. Will rushed right past Abby. "I thought I'd never see you again."

Abby stared. The attractive young woman stepped into those muscular arms with a grin from ear to ear that said all that words couldn't.

Will's cheeks warmed. He had walked right past his parents. And they didn't know anything about Jeannine yet. He'd started writing her after last year's two-week furlough. What must they be thinking? He never mentioned having dated her when he was home. Not one word in all his letters. Why? What had kept him from writing about the love of his life?

His folks stared as Jeannine wrapped around him like an octopus around the hull of a ship. While he didn't exactly mind, he realized how inappropriately they were behaving. He glanced up to see his parents' mouths nearly unhinge. He should have prepared them when he'd written. Now he couldn't very well push her away and peck her on the cheek. He was making it obvious they were an item.

Embarrassed at the display, Will finally pulled back. "Mother, Dad. Over here." He motioned for them to join him. "This is Jeannine Baker. We, uh. We met while I was home last year."

His mother's demeanor tightened. Odd. Well, they would come to love her like he did—in time. They couldn't very well have feelings one way or the other; they didn't know Jeannine. Did they? He couldn't be sure. New Hope being a small town and all. He glanced at Jeannine, hoping she didn't read their unsettled faces as clearly as he did.

His father recovered quickly and held out his hand, gracious as always. "Is she your surprise, son? If so, she's a very lovely surprise." While his words suggested cordiality, he tensed when he reached toward her. Will hadn't seen either of his parents act like this before. His home, his family had always been open and warm to everyone.

Will's head listed to the side. "Not quite *all* my surprise. Only half of it." He released himself from Jeannine's embrace. "Wait here for the other half." Pivoting toward the train where Hank waited, he motioned to the boy. "C'mere, buddy. I want you to meet my folks."

Running the dozen or so steps with almost no wobble now, Hank reached out and his small hand curled into Will's big paw. Lip trembling, he stood as tall as possible and said, "My name Henryk. Hank. I happy to meet you." Then he smiled that endearing grin of his, though

Will realized how difficult it must be to act so brave at only four, and with all these faces locked onto his.

Jeannine sidled forward, a frown firmly planted in place. Oh boy, here it was. All the letters, but no time to write about Hank before he'd left Germany. Somehow he should have made more of an effort; he just hadn't known what to say. In seconds her frown turned to a very strange smile. "Will. What's this darling little boy all about?"

Abby stood aside, soaking in the reunion one emotion at a time. The boy was his surprise. Where had he come from? Such a darling. How on earth had Will taken on the responsibility of a small child? Maybe he was traveling with Will until his parents could arrive, be located. There must be some reason. One didn't randomly pick up a small child on his way back from Europe. Most of the family had lost their looks of surprise and now smiled broadly at Hank.

All except this Jeannine woman who didn't look any too happy as she clutched at Will's elbow. Possession was nine tenths of the law. "Who does he belong to, William?" Her nails dug into his arm, the bright red standing out against his uniform like tomatoes on a vine.

Will's mother stepped forward and scooped the boy into her ample arms. Abby couldn't help but notice how quickly he snuggled in. "Well, whoever he belongs to, we need to fatten him up, now, don't we?" Her hug lasted far longer than the boy's comfort. He wriggled free, looked her in the eyes and returned his gaze to Will as if asking whether or not he'd been dumped on strangers. Poor little tyke.

With the tip of his finger he pointed once again to his chest. "My name is Hank. I happy to meet you."

Mr. Judge offered his hand. "And we're happy to meet you, too, Hank. This is Abigail."

Will spun on his heel, his eyes wide. "Abigail? Barbara's sister? It can't be. Why, she's a spindly little tree scrub about fifteen years old." With eyes twinkling, he clipped her under the nose. "Hey, it is you, squirt. Look at you." His eyes raked her over, their sparkle brighter by the second.

She put hands to her face, covering it as her cheeks warmed under his scrutiny.

Jeannine noticed her, too, only not as cheerfully as Will. But she smiled that forced wide grin and grasped Abby's arm. "So nice to meet one of Will's childhood chums. And his family. What an exciting day this has turned out to be. My, but this is a happy time for all of us now that we have our Will home. Isn't it?" When the others were preoccupied with Hank's antics, Jeannine's lips pursed with displeasure at Abby.

Abby thought if looks could bite, she'd have a dozen fang marks embedded in her skin. But Abby understood the girl's reaction completely. While she, herself, wouldn't mind fighting for this soldier, it was clear: he had a *thing* for the voluptuous redhead. So Abby took her cue to bow out gracefully, leaving him to Miss Phony Smile.

Will zipped around, gathering his duffel bag and the small satchel. "Here you go, buddy. You carry your own bag."

Hank pointed to himself. "Dis my bag. My new clothes. All for me."

As Jeannine grasped Will again, Abby didn't want Hank feeling left out, so she grabbed his hand and walked with him to the car. She glanced out of the corner of her eye and blinked away a tear. Will strolled intimately, arm and arm, with Jeannine Baker.

"Will, honey. Are you watching that little boy for someone? Why is he traveling with you?"

Will dismissed her words, but held her tight to him. He'd waited a very long time for this moment and wasn't going to have it ruined with a foolish disagreement. "I've missed you so much, baby." If she loved him enough, nothing else in the world mattered. Only the two of them.

She screeched to a stop, drawing a hailstorm of unwanted attention. "Will, you didn't answer me. I asked you about that urchin you brought with you."

Straightening, as if the breath had been knocked out of his lungs, Will glared at her. Had she really called Hank an urchin? Strangers or no strangers, they would have this out. "Don't talk about Hank that way. *Don't* talk about him like he's a dog, Jeannine. He's with me. And will be from now on." He grabbed her arm and narrowed his gaze on her, his voice dropping to a whisper. "Hank spent two years in a concentration camp, all because his folks helped some Jewish families escape. Now he gets a chance at a good life. I won't have you persecuting him all over again." Who in their right mind wouldn't want to care for this little boy? His little boy.

Jeannine leaned in, tickling his chin with her curly hair. "I didn't mean that the way it sounded. Don't be mad at me, Willie. Of course he's with you, darling.

We'll talk about that later. There's plenty of time to make important decisions."

Will glanced over at his parents, and then at Abigail—Abby. She had crouched down by the car, tying Hank's shoes with a huge smile on her face, the kind of grin she'd offered him as a kid when she'd thought he wasn't looking. After the ties were tight, Hank wrapped his arms around her neck and kissed her cheek. What had she jokingly called Will? A cousin? Kissing cousins. He gave a quick shake of his head to clear her from his mind.

He doubted Abigail would be up for his kisses. And he was fairly sure Jeannine wouldn't like the idea at all. He glanced back at Jeannine. They'd been writing for a year, and he'd been eager to get home to her. Maybe, in time, she'd realize how important Hank was to him. Of course she would. Who wouldn't love Hank?

She smiled up at him and licked her lips; his anger ebbed.

Well, she'd better get it through her head Hank came with him if they planned to get married this summer. Hank, more than anyone or anything else, was his priority.

"I should go with the folks. I'm sure they've killed the fatted calf."

"The what?"

"You know. The fatted calf, Jeannine. From the Prodigal Son?"

"Oh, that Bible stuff of yours," she replied, her pout obvious to anyone staring. And plenty of folks were staring.

He rubbed the back of his neck and squeezed with tight fingers. "Yeah, that Bible stuff."

"Okay, but don't forget. I expect to see you tomorrow. Bright and early." Her face darkened. "No ifs, ands or buts."

His head spun with the ultimatum. In time he'd have to set her straight, but not here, not in front of his family. "After I get Hank dressed, fed and feeling comfortable with the family. I guess I also have a new niece to meet. So much has happened since I left."

Jeannine snapped back, hands on hips that kept inviting him for another look. "Well, are you *ever* going to have a few minutes for me? I've been waiting an awfully long time, William Judge." She stomped her foot, the flower on her hat bobbing, and then she turned her back. Her posture told him he'd better find time if he knew what was good for him.

Was this really the same girl who had written him such love-filled letters?

The heat outside and the tension inside raised the discomfort level in the car until Abby wanted to jump out and run. Sweat dribbling over her chest and down her back, she shifted toward the open window, begging for a breeze to drift in and soften the intense closeness.

Will's parents had witnessed Jeannine's temper tantrum as had Abby, though she'd tried her best not to stare. Out of fairness, Hank must have been quite a surprise to Jeannine, but any woman would find him simply adorable. Abby couldn't wait to see his eyes light up once they arrived at the Judges' and she brought out the sugar cookies and a glass of ice-cold milk. Poor little punkin. It was evident from his knobby joints he'd been starved. How could they? So precious and sweet, he wrapped her heart in ribbons and bows.

She longed to hear every detail of what had happened, not only to Hank, but to Will as well. His life these past years must have been filled with tremendous challenges. He'd shared a bit in his letters, but not so much it would frighten her. He'd no doubt felt the need to protect *little Abigail Richardson*. That seemed to be how he viewed her. And she didn't begin to comprehend what Hank had endured. For now she needed to put on a pleasant face and make them feel welcome—back to sanity.

She glanced around Hank's head toward the front seat. "We were so happy to hear you'd been found, Will." Happy wasn't a strong enough word. She and Mrs. Judge had nearly sounded the alarm to let everyone know he was accounted for.

He gazed over his shoulder and chuckled. "What? You thought I was lost?" The deep timbre of his voice stirred new feelings in her. What was happening to her? Michael's kiss had given her fewer goose bumps than Will's voice.

"You didn't know?" She felt her eyes grow wider.

He stretched an arm along the seat top and turned with plenty of sass plastered on his face. "Seriously, it's easy to explain. Just a mix-up in orders. But in the end, the military's chaos, and there's always chaos, helped me to keep Hank."

"What happened?"

"Once we arrived back at the camp, mass confusion ensued between sending refugees home, finding relatives, separating our orders to get us to the right places. I'm not sure what I would have done if they'd tried to take Hank away." He reached over the seat and patted the boy's leg. "We're supposed to be together, right, buddy?"

Hank's fists pumped in the air between them. "Righhht, buddy."

Abby tugged the boy close and kissed the stubbled head. Without a blink, Hank brushed the kisses off. "Yuck." But his face beamed in confirmation of his true sentiments. It was probable he hadn't received much in the line of mothering if he and his parents had been separated in the camp. Abby heaved a sigh. They might never know all that had happened to him. And maybe that was for a reason. Sometimes, the least said the best, according to her mother.

Switching to a smile before the little fellow recognized her frustration, Abby allowed tickling fingers to cover his tummy, and to her delight, he didn't try to stop the attack. "Yuck, huh? Yuck?" Abby looked up, out of breath, and caught Will staring at the two of them. Maybe he didn't want her getting Hank all excited. Or to get too close. It was more important that Hank be allowed to adjust to Jeannine, not Abby.

The car rolled into the drive as she pondered all the implications of Will and Hank's future in New Hope. Could Jeannine come around to Will's way of thinking?

Will put her mind to rest when he grinned over the seat at the boy. "Welcome home, Hank."

Between giggles Hank shouted, "Wecomome!"

* * *

As his family piled out of the car, Will did a second, closer inspection of the pesky kid who'd driven him to distraction long ago. Five years had been kind to her. No longer scrawny, not by a long shot, Abby stood nearly to his forehead. Tall and beautiful with thick honey-colored hair and bright blue eyes. She looked a bit like his sister-in-law, Barbara, only much prettier.

Those Hoosiers knew how to raise a fine crop of young women. But he wouldn't say that to Barbara *or* Abby. If Abby proved to be anything like her sister, she wouldn't cotton to the reference one bit. The Richardson women, raised to be very independent by their father, weren't exactly fainting flowers. But he'd known all along she'd turn into a beauty. After all, she'd been wonderful even as a scrubby pest.

"William, I asked you if you had everything?" his mother admonished.

He whipped around. "Oh, sure. Except for this little guy." Will hoisted Hank onto his back and laughed at the high-pitched squeals as they galloped all the way to the house.

Sliding Hank from his shoulders, Will stared at the porch, chuckled at the way the ivy crawled up the pine tree in the front, and he longed to sit in the swing just outside the door. Grateful to be home, he grabbed Hank's hand and walked him toward the kitchen. "I know I don't need to ask, buddy, but are you hungry?"

Inquisitive eyes and a growling belly answered, causing Will's parents to laugh. He'd have to introduce Hank to peanuts. He'd never be hungry again.

At that very moment Barbara turned the corner with

a wooden spoon in her hand. "Just about to ladle up the chicken and dumplings. Do I have any takers?" She stopped short and gasped. "And who's this big fellow?" She dropped to one knee, putting herself at his level. Glancing up, questions danced across her smiling face.

Will returned the smile, knowing Barbara would make Hank welcome. "I'd like you to meet my boy, Henryk Drobinski. I just call him Hank."

Hank's small finger poked his pitiful chest for the sixth or seventh time that day. "I call me Hank. Happy to meet you." A big yawn followed and his hand dropped to his side.

The trip had been long and tiring, and as Hank's eyes began to lose some of their luster, Will sensed the little guy needed sleep far more than food. But the boy had to eat before retiring. As his mother had said, they needed to fatten him up.

Barbara set the spoon on the table and wrapped Hank in her arms. "I'm Aunt Barbara. Happy to meet you, too, Henryk Drobinski."

"I Hank." He nodded, a bit slower this time.

She squeezed. "Okay, Hank. Hungry?"

"Hank hungry." His grin, prematurely missing a tooth in the front—from the malnutrition?—warmed Will through and through. For this child of sorrows to exhibit so much joy after such a short stint at freedom took the heart of a champion. In time Will would tell the family all that had happened to Hank and how he came to be in a concentration camp. He had a proud heritage, one Will intended to keep alive so Hank's parents, heroes through and through, would never die in his memories.

"Where's that niece of mine, Barbara? I've been waiting for Jackson to become a daddy. Not sure, but I think I might have beat him by a couple of days." He laughed out loud at his own joke. "And call me foolish, but I do believe my son is four years older than my niece. How did all this happen?" He winked at Abby and wasn't sure why his heart flipped in his chest at her pink cheeks.

After visiting a few minutes, they all washed up and enjoyed Barbara's cooking. Will hadn't eaten anything so delicious in a very long time. The dumplings were light enough to fly clean off his plate.

And Mother's applesauce? Hank ate half a saucerful of the spicy goodness. He made another half plate of chicken disappear, and then he managed to fit in a small slice of rhubarb pie with a glass of cold milk.

His tummy finally full and eyes growing listless, Hank's head dipped toward his plate a couple of times before the rest of the family finished their pie. Will chuckled. "Look at that. He ate almost as much as I did, but I think it's time to call it a night."

His mother didn't miss the sleepy signs either. "It is time for some little boy to head for bed."

Will offered his best grin. "Still telling me to go to bed, Mother?" He stood and pulled back Hank's chair. "I go from one sergeant to another. And I do believe you're the tougher of the two."

His mother blushed. "You know I meant Hank." How he'd missed her smile, her caring. He couldn't help wondering. Would Jeannine be as good a mother to Hank?

His mother rose and pecked his cheek. "Like it or not, you boys will always be my little boys no matter how big you get."

Will didn't really mind. He hugged her, then turned to Hank. "Guess I'll give him his bath in the morning. He's plum tuckered out." He lifted the exhausted boy into his arms.

"Go on. Just carry him up. While we were visiting, I had your dad move one of the twin beds from Betty's room into yours. Will that be all right? I thought he might be afraid to stay alone for a while. I remember how you kids were in a strange place." She leaned forward, whispering for him alone, but her voice carried. "Your old stuffed pirate is on the bed, too."

Jackson raised an eyebrow and Abby glanced up from her pie. Was that a smirk on her face? No secrets were left now.

"My pirate, eh?" Will's grip on Hank tightened. "Petey the Pirate. Arrrrgh, matey." He glanced Abby's direction. "Well, this is embarrassing. Thanks, Mother." But he chuckled, anyway. No use getting upset when his mother pulled out the memorabilia. As she had proven a few minutes ago, she was Mother after all.

"Petey?" Hank mumbled, his head lolling to the side where Will held it to his shoulder. The warm little body pressed into his, sending protective feelings through Will's arms to the boy. So this is what it meant to be a parent. Experiencing every tear, every joy and every hurt. How he loved Hank. His feelings for his parents had increased so much now that he realized how deeply they cared for all their children. Like when he was small and his mother would say, "Just wait until you have kids of your own."

Will's dad stood, hands sheltering Hank's back in

case. "Need help, son? He must have put on five pounds with that good supper alone."

"I've got him, Dad." Will shifted him against his hip. "Thanks for making him so welcome."

Hank offered a droopy smile and one last sleepy, "Wecomome."

Will took in the family gathering, his gaze coming to rest on Abby. "Thank you, all of you." He shouldn't have doubted their support. It surprised him, though, how Abby had taken to Hank right away, like a mother hen.

His father's forehead creased. "How could we not embrace him? He's a cute little guy."

Should he divulge the whole story? Maybe not all of it—not yet. His mother would have conniptions. She'd likely ride in the belly of a ship to get to Germany and face off with the fellow at the train station. He nearly laughed out loud thinking of the man with his pants tied around his ankles. It was easier now to remember without all the fresh hatred festering. *Thank you, Lord.* "Not only that, Dad. He's much more than just my boy."

His father's eyebrows rose. "How's that?"

He brushed his hand over Hank's sleepy forehead and kissed his cheek. "This little peanut saved my life."

Chapter 4

Two weeks passed with Will opening up a bit more each day about his and Hank's adventure through Germany to the border of Poland. Abby teared up whenever the image slithered through her mind—a small boy, barely old enough to dress himself, certainly not strong by a long shot, swinging a metal pipe to save his hero. Her hero. She gulped back a sob; imagining the worst set her heart throbbing.

If that Nazi had forced Will to go with him, chances were she wouldn't have seen him again. Abby's stomach clenched. If only women ruled the world, they'd put a stop to the nonsense.

Aunt Pearl had told her the big war wouldn't have happened had women been allowed to use the common sense the good Lord had given them. "What's wrong with men? Did the Lord somehow cheat them of a sound brain?" Then she'd laugh with that way about her and roll her eyes.

Abby missed being home with her parents and her aunts. Life in her family never failed to bring laughter. No laughter today. Pondering the possibility Will could have been lost forever, Abby choked on another sob.

But he had returned; they had returned. Will *and* Hank. So why the melancholy?

His heart belonged to another woman.

She should have told him in her letters how she felt about him, instead of prattling on like a child about the new baby on the way and silly stories about her little sister, Dorothy, at home. Yet how could she have known how she would feel once she encountered him face-to-face? Those eyes. Those wonderful, expressive, warm and inviting eyes. Obviously the letters had been nothing more than friendly gibberish to help him pass the time. Pen pals. Ugh. Why had she referred to the two of them as pen pals?

In between the lines, though, she had offered a portion of her heart to the lonely soldier thousands of miles from home. But not everyone read between the lines. She'd learned her lesson with Michael and did her best not to come across as forward, but she might have at least ended her letters with Yours, Abby. That Jeannine girl probably ended her letters with hugs and kisses. Now Abby didn't stand a chance.

With a groan, she scanned her room. Jackson and Barbara had built a lovely home that comforted her. Abby's visit had been extended when Barbara fell and sprained her ankle after she and Jackson had returned home from the main house a week ago. Abby had stayed

on to help care for Barbara. Normally she would love
to stay as long as possible, but now she felt it was a tor-
ture as Will and Jeannine's wedding plans would no
doubt slap her in the face each day. And for good reason. They were in love, happy to share their news with
the family. As part of the family, Abby had no choice.
She would smile and nod and offer words of encouragement when appropriate, but her heart would be breaking every minute.

Oh, Barbara, why did you have to fall? One wrong
step and down her sister had gone protecting her tiny
bundle. Grace had suffered nothing other than a mommy
who had to be more careful. Barbara had a sprained
ankle: black, blue, yellow and swollen the size of a
grapefruit. For five days, Abby had played nursemaid,
and quite well, thank you very much. Icing, stretching,
moving the ankle so it wouldn't grow stiff. She'd spent
her spare moments caring for Grace.

Now that Barbara was managing fairly well on her
own, Abby had been spending a lot more time at the
Judges' helping with Hank. Although maybe the less
time spent at the Judges' the better. After all, she wasn't
being fair to Jeannine. Jeannine had the right to con-
nect with Hank, not Abby.

Her heart clenched with the desire to have a baby of
her own, a baby with Will. How long had this dream
filled her being? A dream it had to remain; Will belonged to Jeannine, not Abby.

She sighed at the reality of the situation and grabbed
a sweater. Then she walked past Barbara and headed
for the front room.

"You going out?" Barbara asked.

"Dishes were done an hour ago. Little Sweet Pea is in the bassinet snoring like her mommy. Thought I'd go for a walk, take in some fresh air. I've felt closed off from the outdoors. You know, like in the winter when the long walks get shorter every day. And now that it's so beautiful out, I want to take advantage of every minute."

Barbara raised a brow and a wicked grin crept over her face. "Why not wander over and check on Hank. He loves when you're around." The expression said far more than her words ever could. Okay, Barbara, time to stop playing matchmaker.

Abby tugged the cardigan-style sweater closer and dropped a frown in her sister's direction. Did her sister read her mind? Her heart? She needed to put a stop to this right now. She scowled at Barbara. "Enough."

"Don't try and stare me down, sis." Barbara leaned against the rocker pillows and chuckled. "Didn't work when we were kids. Won't work now. You like being at the Judges'. I know you do. You've never been good at hiding your feelings from me."

Barbara's smirk irritated the socks off Abby. But she spoke the truth. She'd never been able to fool her sister. "I'm sure I don't have an inkling what you're talking about." If she didn't escape soon, she would have to explain tears, and life was too short to live with tears over situations one couldn't control.

"You're going to see about Hank, of course."

"Naturally I'm only checking on Hank. Mrs. Judge has her hands full with…well, she always has plenty to do. So I thought if I could help, I should." She stuffed her hands into the big pockets of the heavy sweater and plunked onto the chair farthest from her sister. Tears threatening or not, if they didn't have this out, Barbara would bring it up again and again. "Why else would I be going to the Judges'?"

Barbara's eyes scorched her, forcing Abby to look away. After a painfully long silence, her sister's words fell softly between them. "Abigail Richardson, if you don't face up to what you're feeling and tell Will, you might not get a second chance."

"Tell him what?" She couldn't possibly be that transparent.

"How you feel. I know you, little sister. Every time you look in Will's direction, your face betrays you. Everything about you comes alive. It's me, Barbara, remember? The sister who listened to you all the way home after we were stranded in New Hope five years ago. Willie Judge this, and Willie Judge that. You'd have thought instead of a little brat, he was the Prince of Wales or Mickey Rooney. There was a special connection between the two of you. If we hadn't lived so far away, you would have been spending time together. Fishing and eating peanuts. I saw you, both of you, you know. When he tugged your hair, you slapped his hands and your face flamed red. No girl blushes when she hates a boy. She gets even and tattles, or worse, she slugs him. You never were a shrinking violet. I recall plenty of boys who went home crying." She rubbed her ankle.

"I don't know what you think you saw."

"I saw plenty, little sister."

Abby straightened, her chin jutting toward Barbara in defiance, even though her sister spoke honestly. "Saw what?"

"You cried after we left. And you had the toy horse

from his room in your pocket. I noticed you playing with it while you were crying." Barbara straightened in her chair, eyes scrutinizing Abby's every move.

Abby looked away. "Oh, that was a silly crush. And he gave me the horse before I left so I'd have something to occupy my time on the way home."

"Very thoughtful for a boy of fifteen, don't you think? If I'm not mistaken, you didn't throw the horse away."

The toy stood guard on her dresser at home, Will's letters wrapped in ribbon right next to it. "Barbara, stop. This is foolishness talking." *And if you don't quit, I might start crying again. He can't know how I feel. It just wouldn't be right.* Her shoulders slumped, she was resigned to her sister knowing her innermost thoughts. "Besides, he already has a girlfriend and they're practically engaged. You heard him. You know all about it same as I. Will and Jeannine. They've been planning to get married for months."

"He doesn't love her."

"Oh, what do you know?"

"All your letters to me were filled with questions about Will. I don't believe you ever asked about me or Jackson, now that I think about it. I'm not the naive girl I was when I left home, Abby. Getting married adds years of wisdom. And I don't recall you *ever* mentioning that Michael What's-His-Name. He couldn't have meant much."

"Oh, wise one."

"Don't be flippant."

Abby chewed her lip and looked at the floor. "But Barbara, he's enga—"

"He does…not…love her, Abby. I see the way you look at him, but I also see the way he looks at you. Like he's being presented with a hot-fudge sundae for the very first time. When you're with Hank, it's all he can do not to run over and wrap his arms around you. He cares about you a lot, Abby. And I can't believe Mama and Dad raised a fool. You, young lady, are behaving like a fool. They aren't married. They aren't even officially engaged. You would be a fool to keep your feelings from Will. From a man whose only feelings for Jeannine are, well, not the kind of feelings that he talks to his mother about."

If only that were true, she'd fight for him, but she didn't see what Barbara thought she saw. She only saw a man crazy about his little boy and anxious for his fiancée to care. Besides, Jeannine was movie-star gorgeous. All that thick long red hair. And her eyes the color of emeralds. What man would trade all that for mousy Abigail Richardson? "Oh, fiddlesticks, Barbara." Abby huffed a whoosh of air, trying to put a stop to the crazy conversation. This talking romantic nonsense might give her hope, hope she didn't deserve. He belonged to another.

"If someone else told you, someone closer to Will, would you believe him?"

Abby nicked at the piece of lint in the pocket of her sweater. Who else would think the way Barbara did? No one. But Barbara was a romantic, conjuring up things that weren't true. But, of course, she had to ask, "Him who?"

Barbara shifted in the chair, her face streaked and creased with pain. "Jackson is the him who. He told me last night once we'd settled into bed. Said he hoped Will would be smart enough to figure it all out so he could be as happy as we are. He said he can tell Will loves you." Barbara giggled and rolled her eyes for at least the dozenth time that day. "And he's not one to talk about romance. He's more likely to laugh at how Will acts, but he doesn't, not when he mentions your name. Jackson's privy to information we can only guess at."

Abby jumped from her seat and headed for the front door. A quick glance back and she fought the flush covering her face. Barbara was trying to help, but in the end, it would leave Abby with expectations that could never be. "Nonsense! You and Jackson have no idea what you're talking about. He loves Jeannine. He waited a long time to be with her. Let's end all the foolish talk right here."

Sun setting behind her, Abby tapped lightly on the Judges' front door. Peering through the screen, she heard a loud, angry voice. Will on the phone. Talking to whom? She shouldn't eavesdrop, but she found it hard to walk away.

"I told you, Jeannine. I can't help that I don't have a lot of time to spend with you. My dad needs me at the factory. Jack's been waiting for me to return home so he can start his new business. And Dad's had a rough time since he had pneumonia." Silence. "Excuse me? There's nothing wrong with managing a factory. It's what I love. But I'm exhausted. I've been with you the past three days. I need some time to myself. Time for Hank and time to relax."

Abby held her breath as more quiet time passed. An

occasional huff from Will was all that broke the silence. Embarrassed that she'd overheard their conversation, she stepped back. Did Jeannine think she was too good for a factory man? Will would own the place one day. But Abby knew he rolled up his sleeves and worked right along with his men. So, Jeannine didn't like a man with calluses on his hands.

"Jeannine, baby. You have no idea what it was like. I know you worried while I was gone, but your worst worry doesn't come close. And now I need time to see how I fit best in New Hope." A low rumble sounded from his throat. "Don't push me, Jeannine!"

Abby stopped. It would be rude to go in, so she took a seat on the swing outside. Ever since Will had come home, this Jeannine girl had raised a ruckus, pouting whenever he wanted to be with his family. She hated that he was torn between Jeannine and Hank, Jeannine and his parents, and of course, she hated that because of Jeannine he hardly noticed her at all. The phone slammed hard.

She pulled a hand to her chest. What would he think if he found her outside?

And then the door squeaked.

"Hey, squirt." His fingers snapped her on the top of the head. "Hope I didn't bother your peace with my rantings."

With a start, she glanced up. "No. I was just enjoying the night air." Will. So tall and handsome even without his uniform on. A thunk on the head. Not quite the sort of attention she'd hoped for. Oh well, at least he recognized she was alive. "Is Hank asleep yet?"

"An hour ago. I'm afraid he's still feeling the effects

of the time change. That and *somebody's* been working him like a dog. Some strange woman on a mission who's been teaching him English."

Abby giggled. "He's like a little sponge. Whatever I say, he mimics me, so why not teach him all I know? He even plays the game you used to when we were kids. Remember how you would keep repeating everything Dot and I said until we tattled?"

Will groaned. "Was I really so immature five years ago?"

She smiled. Maybe without the language barrier, Jeannine would adjust to Hank more easily and he to her. "English will open all kinds of doors for him. When he starts school, he needs to speak the language well. I won't have children making fun of him."

"*You* won't?"

"Oh, stop. You know what I mean." Had she given herself away? She longed to stay here, be with Will and Hank, help raise the boy. But that was just a dream. Still, her heart would break if kids made fun of Hank. "You wouldn't tolerate that for a second and you know it."

Will eased her aside and sat down. "You've worked miracles and I appreciate it. He actually said most of his prayer tonight by himself."

"Do the Jewish people pray the same way we do?" She understood so little about such things.

His forehead creased. "He isn't Jewish, Abby. Not that it would make any difference to me, but his family didn't get thrown in the camp because of their faith or their bloodlines, they were captured because they'd helped Jews escape in Poland and Germany."

"I didn't realize." She blinked away tears. "They must have been very brave people."

"His mother and father were imprisoned for nothing more than their compassion." Will's fingers tightened into fists. "It was rumored that the Nazis killed his folks for trying to steal extra bread for Hank, but no one knew for sure. I heard that parents were separated from the children upon arrival, so I don't know how they could have gotten bread to him. It's so hard to separate truth from rumor. But other prisoners told me how the Nazis acted with the little ones. The soldiers would eat their rations in front of the children to anger the parents. Then when their folks fought back, the Nazis had a reason to kill them. Not that a reason ever seemed to be needed."

"Oh, Will." Abby pushed the damp hair from her forehead. "I guess I wasn't paying much attention when you talked to us before. Actually, I think I shut my ears. It's all so unsettling to mull over." A person's compassion had imprisoned Hank's entire family. How strange the world had become. An odd, cold, frightful place. "I'm sorry if I didn't listen better. It couldn't have been easy for you to talk about."

"Can't say as I blame you for shutting out the horror of it all." He leaned toward her.

Abby needed space between them. His closeness unsettled her. All this talk about the Nazis' cruelty and Hank's brave parents. Knowing Hank could be harmed, they continued to help the Jews escape. That was certainly living out their faith. "That, and I have trouble keeping my eyes off your little boy, he's so precious." She turned away from Will, hands dancing in her lap. "I don't understand how those soldiers could have been...I just. How can anyone be so cruel?" Will draped an arm across her shoulders.

She closed her eyes for a brief second and allowed his gentle touch to reach her heart. If this was one of the only moments she would have with him, she'd enjoy his closeness to the fullest. Warmth coursed through her. When she opened her eyes, she wondered, did he sense the intensity of their nearness? Could he tell what she harbored in her heart?

He smiled a stiff smile. "It's okay. I feel the same way about how he was treated. I do realize I'm going to have to go to God and learn forgiveness...in time, but that's one of the reasons I couldn't leave him there with no one to take care of him. I keep hoping Jeannine will come around." His eyes locked onto a distant place. He blew out a long breath. "Sure she will, in time. Just has to get over the shock of me bringing Hank home this way with no warning. All women would be surprised, wouldn't they? Abby, please tell me her reaction is normal." He chewed the edge of his lip and glanced at the ground. "Who am I kidding? You didn't act that way when you met Hank. And there's nothing in it for you. Not like we're engaged or anything, just friends, right?" He waited an extraordinarily long moment. "Aren't we only friends, Abby?"

Who was he trying to convince? Maybe she should simply tell him. *I'm crazy about you, Will Judge. Let's not be just friends.* But it wouldn't be fair and she believed in playing fair. She ignored the obvious and returned the conversation to what had to be. "Do you plan on being married soon or are you going to wait a while?"

His hand fell back to the seat, leaving her cold and trembling. "Before I came home that's all I thought about, but now? I'm not sure. Before we can marry, Jeannine must understand that she's getting the whole kit and caboodle. Both me and Hank, that, and I don't think she likes the idea of being a factory worker's wife very much. I'm not certain what all she expected. I was completely honest in my letters about what my plans were when I returned home. I haven't told her the factory will be mine and Jackson's one day. I want her to love me for being an average Joe. Not the owner of a company. Not that it should make any difference in the scheme of things. I plan to be very hands-on in the factory. Always have been, always will."

Abby's cheeks heated up. "What's wrong with running a factory? Or working in one for that matter. If you love someone, the man's job should have nothing to do with it." How dare that girl belittle Will's work. As quickly as she'd said that, she remembered him chomping peanuts. And she giggled.

Will's head cocked to the side. "What's so funny?"

"You and the peanuts. I laughed when I first saw you. So intent on eating every one, I thought you'd burst."

He chuckled and made a face. "Oh, boy. That's exactly how I want you to think of me." He turned a cheek. "Aren't I just a bit more handsome now?"

She ignored the question, convinced she could never tell him how his face drew her in, how each eye creased when he smiled, or how his strength flowed from his muscular stature right through her when he draped an arm across her shoulders. If she breathed one of these sentiments, she might lean closer and kiss him. Right here. Right in front of God and everybody. "Oh, you were such a brat teasing us girls and all."

"*I* was, was I? If I remember right, you and your sister Dot were quite the instigators when it came to trouble. You'd raise havoc and blame it on me, knowing my mother would always believe sweet innocent girls. Does the frozen cherry raid ring a bell? You and Dot ate a whole container and blamed me. Remember? But I couldn't keep my eyes off you. I think at fifteen years old, I was already madly in love." He tugged her to him and tickled her sides like he had when they were younger.

As suddenly as he'd started, he stopped, jerked his hands back and sobered. Abby couldn't tell who was the most startled. He cleared his throat. "I'm sorry. I had no right to behave so. Please forgive me, Abby."

They both quieted, not a sound at all except the loud beating of Abby's heart rushing in her ears. For what seemed like forever, they simply stared at each other. Abby took in every detail of his face, and his eyes roved over her until she wriggled under the scrutiny.

Even the crickets seemed to still. Not a breath of air stirred. Only two faces close as one, not moving an inch. She swallowed hard, holding back every word she longed to say. Perhaps, if she took Barbara's advice and told him how she felt. How she really felt.

No, she pictured Jeannine's face again. She had no right.

At last she backed out of reach and stood. "I guess I'd better go in. It's getting chilly."

Eyes still locked on hers, Will rose slowly, his thigh grazing hers as he stood over her. His arms opened automatically. "Here."

The only word she needed filled her heart. He wrapped her in a tender embrace that left her breathless. His head dipped closer. "Isn't this better?"

Without thinking, Abby leaned her head against his chest, drawing comfort from the warmth and strength of his arms. She'd love him no matter what his circumstances. He could be a rag collector for all she cared. Good job, bad job. Ready-made family, just the two of them. As long as she could stay right here, sheltered in the safety of his arms for as long as they both lived.

Unable to stop the huge sigh, Abby said, "Mmm. Much better, thanks."

He tightened his arms. "Yeah, it is, isn't it?"

But a small voice whispered from her heart to her conscience. A picture of Jeannine crept in, pushing all her comforting thoughts aside and she straightened. These arms around her weren't hers to share. She couldn't do this, wouldn't want some other woman to act this way with her beau. She'd been raised to behave with stronger morals.

She leaned back, gazed into the coffee-brown eyes that had sparkled and teased a few years ago, but now questioned her.

Will's brow deepened. "Something wrong?"

"You're spoken for. This isn't fair to Jeannine."

"But, Abby."

She put fingers to his lips. "Shh. Not another word."

Her heart hammered the familiar rhythm, the one that said she'd been down this path before.

Michael. Only she'd been on the other end. Michael's admonition to her that she was a baby, too afraid to confront her parents had left her questioning all she'd been taught. She had packed her bag and confirmed the time and place with Michael. But when she'd come to her senses and refused to run away with him, he'd left without another word. Within a month he'd married one of her best friends. Another Abigail—how very convenient. No longer one of her best friends, Abigail Hunter now had Michael to contend with, and while the betrayal had hurt at first, Abby had realized the wisdom of what her parents had been saying all along. Michael put up a good front, but he had been a man out for what he wanted, never mind what the girl wanted or who he hurt in the process.

And here she was in the arms of another woman's beau. She pressed his chest with hands that longed to pull him closer and tell him how much she loved him, but they couldn't. She dropped them to her sides and stepped away. "This isn't right, Will. I wouldn't want another girl to hurt me." Her head hung, afraid to make any more eye contact with him. He would be able to read her heart. "It isn't fair to Jeannine."

"Abby."

"No, Will."

He groaned and released her, but found time to peck her on the cheek first. "Just one kiss won't hurt." Will's eyes stared into hers, telling her all she wanted to know. One word would turn him away from Jeannine for good. His embrace had told her more surely than his words all the doubts he was having. More than doubts. "Good night, Abigail."

Abby was right, of course. Will couldn't be a louse to Jeannine. He was better than that. And the two of them had made promises in their letters. He planned to honor those promises. If only…if only he'd met Abby sooner, not as children, but as adults. Her letters were so noncommittal, like a friend, nothing more. But here she was, all grown up and so loving. His heart raced like a locomotive whenever she smiled at him. While undeniably beautiful on the outside, her inner beauty shone in the little ways she made him feel important, made Hank feel safe, made his family feel cared for. Had he really been taken in by Jeannine's looks alone?

When Abby played with Hank, he didn't hesitate, didn't show any uncertainty and Will understood how important that was for Hank to move forward. If Will and Jeannine married, would she eventually warm up and want to be a mother to Hank? All women wanted children, right? Mothering came naturally to them—or did it? Abby was a natural, for sure. But Jeannine. He hoped Abby was right about her coming around.

He rolled over in bed for what he prayed was the last time. A quick glance at the clock said he'd been trying to fall asleep for over two hours—too much running through his head. His fingers tugged through his military cut. In all fairness, he hadn't really given her much of a choice. He supposed any young girl just eighteen years old would be as unsure of herself. He'd wait, give her a chance to grow accustomed to the idea, and then he'd know in his heart if they could work out as a family. No rush to the altar made sense at this point. He'd take his time and allow Jeannine to do the same. After all, she loved him. Didn't she?

The most important thing right now was to set actions in motion for him to adopt Hank. He couldn't look to his parents or Jack and Barbara to adopt the boy, and anyway, he wanted to be Hank's father, not just a big brother. The adoption would probably take all the money he'd saved, but so what? After all Hank had been through, Will had to claim his boy. This was what Will wanted more than anything else in the world. Even more than Jeannine. And *nothing* would prevent him from becoming Hank's father.

Chapter 5

"Oh, Will. I'm so happy for you." Abby dipped her hand in the pan of water and sprinkled, then rolled Hank's little shirts for ironing. She wedged them into the basket along with the rest of the clean laundry she would iron later. If she kept busy, she wouldn't so easily allow her thoughts to go to the two of them. "So, it's official. Are you going to celebrate?"

A lopsided grin followed his good news. "Yeah. Mother said she'd cook up a fancy dinner for all of us. A shindig, I think she said."

"I can imagine that's exactly what she said." When she smiled, he seemed to brighten. His hands twitched at his sides as if he might grab her and explore their feelings further. *No, that wouldn't be right.* She stepped back, putting distance between them. If she had to be the one to steer them away from each other, then so be it.

Instead he shook his head and leaned in, whispering, "By the way, you two are the only ones who know what my *big news* is, so don't tell anyone. Jeannine's coming, too." His eyes clouded, but the smile returned right away as he folded two pairs of overalls. "Are you sure these don't need ironing?"

"No. That's wasted time. One minute out the door and he'll have them all dirty and wrinkled. They're meant to be played in. Although if my mother had the smallest inkling I didn't plan to starch and press them, she would be scandalized. She'd iron my father's socks if she could figure out a way to do it." She smiled to think of her mother's thoughts on the subject.

Soon Will might have to get the hang of being mother as well as father. Because she doubted very much Jeannine was the type to worry about whether or not to iron socks. But who knew, she might come around and be a wonderful parent for Hank. Stranger things had happened.

Will stepped closer, laid a hand on Abby's arm. "I can't thank you enough for all you've done for us. We'd have survived, no doubt, with Mother hovering, but you made Hank's shift from prison to family life much easier. And he's learned so much English. How you did all that, I'll never know."

His fingers worked their way down her arm and he rubbed the back of her hand with his thumb. His fingers, callused from hard work, felt like a river of fire wherever his touch landed. Her breath caught in her throat and she closed her eyes. Little ripples of warmth coursed up and down her arms until Abby could think of nothing else. Until. Jeannine's face intruded. His fiancée pushed, unwelcome, into her mind. Again.

Beautiful, voluptuous Jeannine.

Abby jerked back so suddenly, the laundry basket upended, clothes in a damp clump. "I—I'm-mm. Sorry." She glanced at her hand where the memory of his touch lingered. "I seem to be all thumbs today." *He needs to leave.* "I'd better get back to work. There's so much to do. Barbara will no doubt need my help before the day's over. Don't you have to go to the factory? The boss shouldn't be late." *Stop rambling. Just pick up the clothes and stack them in the basket. Don't let him see you flustered.* If that were the case, he wouldn't be able to see her—ever. She always seemed flustered when Will was around.

Will ran fingers over his head. "Plenty of work for me there, but I think I'll spend some time with Hank first." He clipped the end of her nose. "One of the benefits of being the boss. Guess it's better if I'm out of your hair, right? Don't forget. Supper tonight is going to be spectacular."

Her arm continued to tingle as Abby chewed her lower lip, planning how to get out of dinner tonight. The news sounded wonderful, but would everyone be as thrilled as Will? Mostly she dreaded the idea of sitting through a family dinner with Jeannine there. Seeing the other woman next to Will caused her heart to plummet into her stomach. How would she ever survive an entire meal with Jeannine dangling on his arm, hanging on his every word? *Willie, honey, look at me and Willie, honey, aren't I just wonderful? Willie, honey, do you really need to keep that little street urchin and his dirty ways?* What had possessed him to ask Jeannine out in the first place? They were nothing alike. Abby didn't believe Will was shallow enough to fall for a pretty face only; So why the attraction? Loneliness? How could he be lonely in this family?

Arms overflowing with laundry, Abby stopped and peeked out the window. Will had Hank on his shoulders, the boy's skinny legs dangling while he clutched at the "horsey's" neck. If a woman could pick an amazing sight that would fill her heart and make her long for the arms of the man she loved all at the same time, it would be this. Any man who could love a child the way Will loved Hank deserved a full life. Those two spent so much time together, she sometimes felt one started where the other finished. If Will wasn't allowed to officially adopt Hank, Abby imagined all types of horrible scenarios for the child. And for Will. He loved that boy more than a natural father in many ways. No doubt because Hank had saved his life. In her wildest dreams she couldn't put together how that must bind the two.

She balanced the clothes basket against the window frame and with another glance between the lace panels, her face warmed to a wave from Will. Did he have the smallest idea how his smile burrowed under her skin? How his deep voice sent shivers along her spine? She couldn't kid herself any longer. This man, without even trying, was breaking down all of her good intentions.

Leaning closer to the window, she made out a wistful cry. "Miss Abby, you walk wif us, puhlease?" Hank's words invited her along and wrangled her heart with little effort.

She opened the door to the sight of both boys, faces pouting. "Puhlease," Will added, a wink the only difference between the two. "You walk, Miss Abby?" His brush cut had started to grow just slightly since coming home. And the brown hair made his eyes that much darker, drawing her in whenever he winked at her. Not able to help herself, she glanced from his eyes, to the broad shoulders that held Hank, to the narrow waist. A waist his mother was doing her best to thicken.

She giggled and put her mind back on business. How could she say no to an invitation like that? She called out, "Let me put the laundry away and grab a sweater." The clean smell of fresh laundry reminded her she shouldn't be playing hooky, but she simply could not resist.

Will tossed Hank in the air as their faces lit up. *Puhlease?*

Hank landed with a thunk against Will's chest and he buried his face in the shoulder that Will knew spelled safety for his little guy. Arms clutching Will like a baby monkey, the boy wrapped his legs tightly and sighed. "You love Hank, Vill?"

Did he ever. What a question. "I love Hank. More than there are clouds in the sky."

Hank's gaze rose, his round eyes wider than usual. "The sky?"

"Yeah, like this." Prying the grasping fingers away, another toss in the air sealed their relationship for a few minutes until Hank would ask again and Will would repeat the toss. He understood it would take time before Hank fully realized Will's love was here to stay without soldiers waiting in the background to take him away. How many cruel pranks had been played on the boy?

Had they allowed him to be with his parents? Will might never know the extent of Hank's horror in that camp, but he could be sure to make Hank's future wonderful.

Hank grasped Will tighter, snuggling into the safe haven. Will eyed him and noticed startling changes.

The boy had begun to fill out, look more like a child his age. Dark brown hair had lengthened and was filling in the bare spots malnutrition had caused. His eyes, a deep brown, were like the chocolate Hank loved so much. Will and Hank looked enough alike, they might be brothers. Better yet, father and son.

Hank's toothless grin only reinforced what Will already knew. He would do whatever it took to keep Hank, to give him the kind of home every boy deserved. A warm place to sleep, enough food to eat and a friend to love him unconditionally. Eventually school, so the little guy's prospects would hold good opportunities. He'd see to it Hank had every advantage Will could afford. While he couldn't make up for Hank's losses thus far, he could ensure the rest of the boy's life held promise.

Over Hank's shoulder Will observed Abby dashing out the door. Light brown hair blowing, eyes bright and full of adventure, and a smile to make any grown man fall to his knees and pledge his love. He shook his head, had to stop thinking of her that way. He'd already promised himself to another. But if he loved Jeannine with every ounce of caring in him, why did his heart beat wildly in his chest whenever Abby neared? His hands grew clammy, his pulse jumped, his eyes stared like a kid with a crush for the first time. And he'd caught himself stammering on two different occasions, no doubt sounding like the town fool.

William Judge. Strong soldier, soon-to-be father, stuttering like a boy in junior high school. How had that happened? Well, no more.

"Hey, there. How are my two favorite men?" She wrapped her arms around Hank but got hands full of Will as well.

There it was again. His skin prickled where her soft fingers touched him. This had to stop. A man could only take so much. And when had he started doubting his feelings for Jeannine so strongly?

He cleared his throat. *Think of something else. Anything else but Abigail. Bricklaying, well digging, sodbusting, any thought at all that will keep her at bay.* Stepping out of her grasp, he gestured toward the field behind the factory. "I thought a walk through the meadow. Maybe pick some wildflowers for the table." Or maybe they should just go home where he could hide out and not have to face her. Better yet, go home and take her in his arms, tell her about his doubts and the new feelings he'd begun to have. How he wanted her to be part of his and Hank's lives.

Then he remembered—Jeannine. A heaviness came to rest on his chest, not Hank's clutching, but an emotional weight that dragged the life out of him. He looked at Abby.

"Wildflowers sound wonderful. Let's go." That smile again—not helping. She stepped in to lift Hank down and took one hand while Will took the other. Together they walked along a dirt path, swinging the boy between them.

"Whoa. More, Abby. More Vill. Whoa. This fun!" His laughter rang between them. "Agin, agin."

Abby stopped every couple of minutes to pick flowers. Will swallowed hard. He hadn't realized how difficult it would be to spend time with her and Hank together—like a family. His gaze took in the way the slight breeze whispered through her hair, lifting the edges enough for him to see her creamy neck. Errghh.

After forcing himself to quash his sentiments, he concentrated on being with a friend. Nothing more. Once his feelings were under control, the afternoon passed leisurely, Abby animated whenever the topic of Grace or Hank came up. There was no doubt to anyone observing her that she had an incredible way with children.

Then out of the blue, like a locomotive, Will's feelings steamed up, surged forward, until he couldn't easily put them to rest. She would gaze his direction, and the entire process of control and lack thereof started all over again.

"Lookit. Lookit the colors!" Hank's arms filled with wildflowers as he ran through the field, picking first one then another.

Abby's eyes lit up when Hank dashed to her side, slipped into her arms, kissed her cheeks and hugged her. She was a natural. Would Jeannine develop these motherly instincts? Perhaps, in time, once she had babies of her own. But what about Hank? He needed a mother. If Jeannine wasn't able to be that for Hank. What then?

Chapter 6

A tired little boy slipped between the crisp sheets in Will's bedroom. Abby settled him in for his nap and his eyes closed the second his head hit the goose feather pillow. Dark circles, leftovers of his incarceration, no longer defined his face. His cheeks had stopped sinking in with each breath. Instead the tiniest fat pads now covered the cheekbones until he looked a bit more like a normal child. And his arms grew stronger every day. The bony protrusions with that sickly skeletal impression he'd had when he'd first arrived had vanished. Abby smiled at the difference a month meant. Mrs. Judge's cooking no doubt.

After cracking the window open, she smoothed the quilt over his legs and tucked it under his feet. What had his bed been like in the camp? A wooden pallet? A scrap of blanket on a floor? Or had he been lucky enough to sleep between two other prisoners where he gleaned body warmth? Perhaps it was better not dwelling on things she couldn't change. Her heart broke simply imagining the horrors he'd endured. Knowing the truth would only be worse. She had to face the fact he might want to talk about it one day. Or not. But, of course, that would be Will and Jeannine's problem. Not hers.

Eyes filling, Abby tiptoed from the room. She whisked away the drops so no one would see. Closing the door, she backpedaled. And turned into a solid chest. Will. A sigh ripped from her throat. He needed to go to work and allow her the peace to sit and patch her wounds. Her heart. But how does a woman patch the hole? She needed Will to fix it, only she wouldn't ask. That was unfair.

"You okay?" He grabbed her shoulders to steady her. His strength ran along her arms and left her fingertips, which twitched from the contact.

"Sure." No, not one bit. "Just thinking what a terrible life Hank left to be with you. He's a lucky little boy, Will. To have you, I mean."

Will cleared his throat. A strange contemplative look swathed his face. "If truth be known, I'm the lucky one. The blessed one. If it hadn't been for Hank, I'm convinced that soldier would have killed me. And even if Hank hadn't saved me, how could I have left him there with the Germans, anyway? How could I have known which ones were good people and which ones had just pretended they didn't know what went on inside Dachau? There *was* no one else to take care of my special little guy."

His tenderness toward the boy overwhelmed her. She

pictured Hank alone and lost. Then she gazed into Will's eyes, so full of compassion. She bit the edge of her lip, causing pain enough to try to stop her feelings was all she really wanted to do.

Without thinking, Abby reached out, put a hand to the side of Will's face, then leaned forward and kissed his cheek. "You're pretty special, yourself."

Dinner couldn't have been more uncomfortable if Will's mother had sat Jeannine and Abby next to one another. Will groaned. All through the cream of celery soup Jeannine had pouted in Abby's direction, unless of course, she saw Will looking her way. Then her face would fan out in a huge smile. Another quick peek out of the corner of his eye told Will the situation wasn't going to get better anytime soon. Had he so misjudged the beautiful redhead? And what could he do about it without raising a ruckus? He dipped his head and addressed the soup spoon instead of worrying about how Jeannine felt about Abby, her feelings out of his control.

As the meal progressed, he watched Abby's demeanor go from the feisty squirt he knew, to a girl unsure whether or not she should openly converse. Whenever a question was posed, Abby looked directly at Jeannine as if she didn't have a right to answer. Her personality didn't generally bow to others. Why did she act like a second-rate citizen? This situation had to be sorted through, but tonight wasn't the time or place. There were enough sour faces at the table, no need to add to the mix.

By dessert Will debated whether or not making his announcement was a good idea. With the last bite of coconut cream pie he heaved a sigh and stood to his feet. He glanced around the table going from his father to his mother. His gaze shifted briefly to Jackson and Barbara, but came to rest between Hank and Abby. First looking at one and then the other.

Jeannine's response was immediate and no doubt intended to draw his attention away from Abby. "Gracious, Will. You look so serious. Why don't you sit back down and finish your coffee?"

Had his groan been audible after her words? He wasn't sure. He only knew he had to step up and be heard. No time like the present. *Please, Lord. Let everyone receive this in the spirit of caring.*

Lifting a spoon, he tapped the edge of his glass. "Well, I know I told you all this was intended as a celebration dinner." He only hoped they'd all see his news the same way he did.

Hank glanced up, coconut cream on his chin, milk moustache under his nose, looking every bit the adorable munchkin. Will's heart soared. This *was* the right decision.

"I've talked with Judge Miller." His palms suddenly grew sweaty as he took in the different expressions. He set the spoon down before it slipped out of his fingers. "And he told me," he took a deep breath, "he'd help me start the adoption process for Hank."

Another pause as he expected his brother and sister-in-law, at least, to burst into applause, but no one said a word for the longest time. Were they saying this was a bad idea, good idea? Checking the expressions one by one, he couldn't tell. Six unhinged jaws didn't give him much insight.

Then Jeannine recovered and sliced through the silence. "You what? Willie, honey, without talking to
me?" All sense of phony smiles ceased right away. "How
could you even consider an important step like adopting Hank without our discussing it? I might not *want*
that kind of responsibility yet."

Enough, Jeannine. That's all he'd heard since he'd
come home. What Jeannine wanted. Never once had she
asked him what he wanted. "I don't see there's much
choice at this point. And to be honest, even if there were,
I'd still be adopting Hank."

"But Will."

He pulled her to her feet, his gaze darting from her to
Hank's bewildered expression and back again. "Now's
not the time, Jeannine."

She bit her bottom lip, chin trembling. Frightened
or angry? "Not the time! Are you teasing me?" She
glanced at the floor as if deciding how much to say in
front of his family. "You should have talked to me, William Judge." Tears dribbled from her eyes. She tugged
a hankie from her pocket and dabbed them. "This just
isn't right."

Will noticed his father's brow rise slightly. He imagined what his father would have to say after dinner about
Jeannine's behavior in front of the family. In front of the
boy. His father, a good and fair man, had taught Will
to be the same. However, and this was a huge *however,*
Will had also been taught to speak up for himself in
every circumstance.

Hank in the meantime had jumped from his seat,
run around the table to Will and Jeannine and wrapped
coconut cream fingers around their legs. Jeannine

screamed. Hank jerked back, eyes filling almost immediately with tears. Will shouted. Seeing the hurt look on Hank's face, he had to force himself not to throttle her. Abby overturned her chair moving to Hank's side where she pulled him into her arms.

A really wonderful celebration dinner.

Jeannine swung around, her face suddenly devoid of tears, but contorted with plenty of anger. "Oh, sure. Little Miss Goody-Goody makes points with Will by taking care of the orphan." As the words left her lips, she gazed about the table, soaking in the looks from Will's parents and his brother and sister-in-law. Her lips tucked in making her look like she was trying to take back the diatribe. But it was too late.

Will understood in that moment that someone else lived behind the gorgeous eyes that didn't seem so beautiful just then. Only a great imitator could so hurt a little boy who had done nothing but try to hug her. They might have married as soon as he'd returned. Thankfully he'd learned in time. Now he had to set things straight.

He grabbed her wrist. "Let's go out on the porch. You're right, Jeannine. We need to talk. Now."

Jeannine tugged Will's arm to her side, clutching and clawing as if this were her only chance to explain. "But, Willie. I just meant—"

"I know exactly what you meant. Mother, Dad, I'll see you folks in a while. I'm sorry dinner ended this way." He pushed his shoulders back and turned to Abby with a smile he understood must appear strained. "Could you get Hank's bath started? I'll be in shortly."

Abby's hold on the boy tightened. Hank's face questioned what had happened, but Will couldn't deal with it right at the moment. "Of course. Let's go, Hank." Abby lifted him into her arms and marched toward the stairs.

Guiding Jeannine outside, Will nudged her in the direction of the swing. "Shall we sit or remain standing?"

Her attempt at a smile faded as they sat down with no one around to watch. When she looked up, her face registered a bitter personality her letters hadn't hinted at. How easy it was, far away from home, to be deceived. And he had been at the head of the line.

"We'll get one thing straight before you say another word, William. I'm eighteen years old. I don't intend to become a mother that soon. You never wrote about Hank, didn't say a word until he showed up on your folks' doorstep, and now you expect me to marry you and be his mother? Why, I have living to do. I can't be tied down with a child."

Head hanging at the truth in her words, he admitted, "You're right. I should have told you. There was a very small window of time for me to write you about any of it, but that's no excuse. I had no right to assume you would be as excited about Hank as I am." But who wouldn't be drawn to the happy face and courage of the boy?

She reached for his arm, hauling him toward her again. "There now. Apologizing wasn't so hard, was it? I'm sure we'll find a wonderful family who will love to raise that precious little boy in there. Why he's so smart and clever and—"

"What?" His breathing stopped. He couldn't speak. Did she really think he was buying her load of manure?

The stink ran thick and deep and all he wanted was to disappear.

She continued, "Why, he'll be a loving son to a nice couple who can't have babies of their own. You just wait and see, Will. We'll find him a perfect home. Aren't you glad we talked about this? Just the two of us without anyone else getting in our business?" Her touch repulsed him in a way he'd never dreamed possible. "I'll have Mother start getting the word out right away."

He turned resigned eyes her direction, not resigned in agreement, but in that he had finally come to realize who she truly was. "He's not a puppy, Jeannine. One doesn't simply put out a sign advertising a son. Free to a good home. Maybe we could drop him off at the pound, right?" He pushed her hand away. "Listen, I have every intention of raising Hank myself. I thought you and I had similar dreams. That you wanted to get married."

She pouted her lips until he was all the more convinced he was doing the right thing. "I do, Willie. You know I want to marry you. Only you."

"I'm not looking for a home for him. He has one already."

Jeannine pulled away. Sat hard against the swing back. "We should be able to get married and have some fun. You just got home from war. I'm anxious to set up a home, have friends over, enjoy our families. A young married couple. I am not going to be a mother this young. And I most certainly am not going to be a mother to that brat!"

Will yanked her shoulder and drew her close to his face. "I don't expect you to be anything to *Hank*. Or to me. I felt obligated to see this through after all the plans we'd made, but Jeannine, we are unequally yoked. This marriage would never work."

Her brow lifted. "Unequally yoked? Is that more of your Bible stuff?" Her arms folded across her chest.

"Yes, that's more of my Bible stuff." His anger spiraled out of control and he had to draw in a deep breath to fight the emotions. "Bible stuff." He hunched forward, his palms resting on the seat of the swing. *Help me with some "Bible stuff," Lord, before I say or do something unkind.*

"You really listened in Sunday school, didn't you?" Jeannine's disdain for his faith became so evident. How did a woman with good parents, a comfortable life and with looks like a model have such a hard heart? What caused her to see the bad in situations instead of striving for the good? Her letters certainly spoke of a different person. A positive person, a happy person, but here was Jeannine, stunning on the outside, stunted on the inside.

Will shifted in the porch swing, uncomfortable for so many reasons. "I s'pose I did listen on Sundays. Didn't seem to be anything wrong in that. In fact, I enjoyed the classes. My faith is what kept me alive in Germany when I thought all was lost."

"Mama Judge's baby boy. Oh, so good."

Will's jaw tightened as he leaned his weight onto his hands and rose. "I'll walk you home."

Jeannine jumped to her feet and huffed. "Don't bother!"

"I can't let you walk alone at night."

She tossed long hair over her shoulder and drew her neck up as high as it would go. "I'd as soon walk with a snake. That's it. You're a snake and I'm lucky I didn't get mixed up with a *boy* like you. Mama told me I didn't know enough about you. I'll bet she'd be surprised to know you and your family are high and mighty. I don't know what I ever saw in you. Love is blind, I guess."

"I guess it is at that."

"Well, no more. You've opened my eyes to who you really are." Turning, she walked across the porch. "I'm safer walking alone than with a hypocrite like you."

Don't be rude. Don't say anything unkind. Just get her out of your life and good riddance!

Will sat down again, his muscles relaxing for the first time since he'd been home. Her footsteps clacked hard on the sidewalk and her purse swung back and forth in rhythm with her heated steps. Suddenly, realizing how grateful he was that he'd avoided a lifetime of unhappiness, he bowed his head. *Thank you, God. For watching out for me even when I didn't know I needed watching over. Now, maybe I can truly begin my life with Hank.*

He had to be honest with himself. Since seeing Abby at the train station, his thoughts had not been wholly on Jeannine. Then when Jeannine made it clear how she felt about Hank, his love for her had done a complete turnaround. If he hadn't felt obligated, he'd have ended this sham of a relationship a couple of weeks ago. Thank God he found out in time. He might have married her, allowed Hank to be mothered by her. What a travesty that would have been.

A breeze whispered over the porch. It felt good sitting here, especially without her lips flapping nonstop, belittling him and his family word after word. The breeze whisked through his hair, cool and inviting after the warm day. He ran fingers over his head and they came to rest in the back. He cracked his neck, breathed a cleansing sigh and closed his eyes. All the letters she'd written suddenly became blank sheets of paper as if she'd not scribbled a word. Because they had all been lies. How fooled he'd been. His father, when giving him *the talk* about women, had warned him about girls who wanted only what benefited them in life. They might be fun to be around, but it was best to keep a distance. They didn't make good wives and mothers. And he'd thought his father was old-fashioned. Didn't understand how the world was changing. A whoosh of air escaped his lungs.

Honey-colored hair filled his mind. Eyes bluer than the lake eased his pain. He listened carefully to the night sounds, but the one that stood out was the soothing voice floating out the bathroom window singing "Oh where oh where has my little dog gone?" He pictured her rubbing bubbles through Hank's hair, scrubbing his skin pink. Laughing, kissing the boy's nose only to hear "yuck" and then kissing him again. Will's lips puckered of their own accord. He envied that lucky little boy.

Oh where oh where had his lovely Jeannine gone? She'd been replaced with a snarling bulldog. He shook his head. No, for the right man, she might be the right woman. But the two of them had different goals, different ways of viewing life. She wasn't a horrible creature, but she wasn't *his* creature. A chuckle bubbled out of his belly. Better not use that expression around Abby.

Chapter 7

Had he sucked his thumb in prison? Abby sat next to Hank's bed, watching him sleep, watching his chest rise and fall, imagining all kinds of horrors the boy must have endured. As deep sleep set in, his thumb slipped from his mouth in a puddle of drool, but his lips continued their sucking motion. His face, that of an angel, made her wonder. Who had cradled his head? Washed and dressed his scrapes? Had anyone cared when he'd cried in the night after a bad dream? Every child should have someone to care when he went from baby to little boy.

Abby's eyes filled. Her heart felt as if it were in a prison of its own, fighting for release. This child had already lived through more heartache than most adults she knew. *God, why? Why would a child so sweet and loving have to live through the terrors of a concentration camp? Be systematically starved? Lose his parents*

*at such a young age? Please help me to understand why
You allowed it.*

She had to do this right, not sound like a whining
child not getting her own way. Dropping to her knees
aside his bed, Abby bowed her head.

"Father, I ask You for Your loving hand to cover this
child with protection. Lift him above the hatred. He has
a wonderful man to father him, Lord. Allow him to
see that. To feel Will's love for him. Help him to grow
strong and sure in spite of having been starved for so
long. Allow him the forgiveness that will set him free
of the past hurts. And help me to understand as well,
Lord, so I might forgive, too."

A hand touched her shoulder and she started. Turning, she met liquid eyes, brown and full of compassion.
"Will?" How long had he been standing there?

"I hope I'm not intruding. I heard you in here and
came to see if you needed my help with Hank. But I can
see you know your way around a little boy. He's lucky
you were here visiting when he arrived. And you're
right, the kind of help he needs will only come from
God. I can't change what happened to him, but I can
help direct the rest of his life. For a while, anyway."

Abby stood and reached behind her back, her hands
intertwining. "Is everything all right with you and…
Jeannine?"

The compassion in his eyes faded and they darkened. "Can we talk outside? I wouldn't want little ears
to overhear."

He tucked her hand into his arm and, together, they
walked downstairs. Will lifted her creamy white sweater
from the hat tree and tossed it over his shoulder. He in-

dicated the door and they strolled outside. Stars sparkled across the sky, large and bright, as if they could be reached and pulled down to illuminate their path. A sudden memory from long ago reminded her how beautiful New Hope appeared at night. Better than in the city where she'd grown up; too many lights blocked the beauty of the night sky. Here a person could see the clear sky for miles in any direction and stars put on a brilliant show each night. She smiled as a shooting star lit up the sky to the west. She closed her eyes and made a wish, like when she was a child. She didn't believe in such foolishness as wishing on a star, but it was fun. And the tail of the star trailed long and low.

Abby shivered in the crisp air, wrapping her arms across her chest.

"You're cold," Will said. "Here, I grabbed your sweater."

"Thank you. I'm not really cold. Well, some, but mostly, it's the thought of Hank in that camp. I can't stop thinking about what happened to him. I fear my imagination might be my undoing. My blood feels like thousands of tiny icicles flowing through my veins whenever I worry about what he must have gone through. Not knowing, I imagine the worst, I'm sure."

"Don't, Abby. You do him no service by linking him to that past. As he grows older, he'll address the issues on his own and I'll listen. Not today, not tomorrow, probably not for a long time yet. We'll help him the most right now by showing him a better life."

"You and *Jeannine* will show him a better life. When you two get married, you'll all settle in. A cozy little family like Barbara and Jackson. Only you'll have Hank to make it better yet. You won't have to wait for a family. I hope she realizes how very lucky she is."

Will's face clouded. His hands shook and he turned away from her. She wasn't sure what she'd said wrong. "Are you all right?"

"There isn't a Jeannine and me any longer."

"There isn't?" Had she heard right? She longed to wrap her arms around him, but suddenly shy, she simply stood there staring.

"No, and I have to think of Hank first. She didn't want to be part of my life with him. I'm afraid I learned a great deal about Jeannine that I hadn't known before. Probably a bit more than I wanted to. In fact—"

"Don't, Will. You did what you had to do." Placing her hand on his arm, she did her best not to shake. Whatever had happened, Will was hurting. "I'm sorry. I know you cared for her a great deal."

He spun around, looked her in the eyes. "I thought I did. When we wrote all those letters making plans for our future, she appeared to want the same things I wanted. A solid marriage. A family. A loving home and, I thought, a house full of children. Now I'm not sure that was ever what Jeannine had in mind. I'll probably never know."

It would be so easy to manipulate Will while he hurt, but she couldn't. Jeannine might have, but Abby understood he had to grieve. "Maybe in time she'll come around."

"No!" He strode across the porch, landing on the other side where his face was hidden in complete darkness. "I won't pretend she's the person I thought she was. Jeannine could never be a mother to Hank, and therefore, she could never be my wife."

Abby watched his shoulders slump, his anger ebbing or increasing. She didn't know him well enough yet to tell. But she did realize he was in pain.

"The strange thing is, I'm not all that sorry." He faced her again, his hands out to the sides. "I should be. Shouldn't I? I mean, if I really and truly loved her, I ought to be feeling some kind of loss in my heart. But there's nothing inside except anger that she could be so callous where that little boy is concerned. And Abby, I'm tired of feeling angry. I've had my fill of anger."

"With Jeannine?"

"Not only Jeannine. When I saw those prisoners before we released them, I was furious enough to kill the first German that crossed my path. I wanted to. I really wanted to. I can't say what I would have done had I been given the chance. I only know what I felt at that moment, especially after finding Hank. War is hard, Abby. It's not news clips before a movie or medals sent home for safekeeping. War is every bit the nightmare that only whispers truthfully in the dark. I have a great deal of anger inside and I'm not sure what I'll do with it yet."

Abby stepped over the worn boards until she stood closer by his side where heat radiated off him. "Don't beat yourself up. I'm sure it's natural to feel that way."

"You have no idea what I imagined myself doing. I have trouble admitting it to God, let alone you or my family. Sleep comes at a cost every night. Many times I don't sleep at all. I simply lie in bed, listening to the ins and outs of Hank's breathing, grateful to God that He saved the boy. His slumber in my room is my one saving grace. He doesn't cry anymore. He sleeps quietly, surely, as if he knows I'll always be there for him. He's still my saving grace."

Would he want her reassurance right now? She took his hand. His warmth crept up her arm, across her shoulder and landed gently in her heart. With one word of encouragement she'd step into his arms and hold him closer than what she thought humanly possible, but his pain left a gap between them that words of comfort couldn't bridge. "Will?"

Brokenhearted eyes gazed at her, through her, until she released his fingers from her grasp. "Are you going to be all right?"

"I'm fine. I'd just like to be alone, I guess. I thought my life was mapped out. And all I had to do was come home and start this perfect family. Now?" Pain fanned across his face, dulling his eyes. "Now I'm starting all over again, and this time, with a son."

Abby kissed the tips of her fingers and touched his lips. "Good night, Will." There had to be a way to show him how much people admired him. "You're a good man."

A good man, huh. A good man would have been able to make Hank *and* Jeannine happy. Now what? As Abby stepped through the front door, he sank onto the porch rail and dragged his palm up the back of his neck. Everything he thought to be true had turned out to be a lie. A year of letters, a year of plans, a year of waiting to return home to…whom? Jeannine? If Jeannine had loved him, truly loved him, she would be here right now helping him orchestrate Hank's adoption. Planning their wedding. Learning to get to know the little boy who would become her son. If…if…if. He remembered the lieutenant shouting at one of his buddies caught sniffling over a Dear John letter.

"What if she loved me. What if I could go home. What if…what if…what if. There's no room for what-ifs in war, soldier. Get over it, move on, remember she wasn't worth it."

Tonight had been a big surprise, all right—a surprise for him. He wasn't even sure his family supported his idea of the adoption, though he understood they would be behind him all the way. What did Mother always say? "As long as it isn't immoral or illegal, we'll support you in anything, now won't we?" And they always had.

Since it was neither of those things, he counted on her being true to her word as usual. Perhaps they weren't falling all over themselves so they wouldn't be disappointed if the adoption didn't go through. Or maybe they were weighing his relationship with Jeannine. Wanting him to marry her or not. He couldn't be sure.

Well he wasn't about to let Jeannine's betrayal stop his plan. First thing tomorrow morning he would pay a call to Judge Miller. No matter what this took, he *would* become Hank's father. Legally. Emotionally was inconsequential; the boy already owned his heart.

Chapter 8

Judge Miller peered over a pair of reading glasses thick as ice on the lake. His brows, wiry and full, bobbed up and down as he squinted. Looking first at Will, then at the paperwork, then at Will again, he finally said, "Whatever possessed you to bring a boy back from Germany in the first place?"

Will cleared his throat. If he tried to speak now, with the emotion behind his words, he would sound like a rambling fool. *The Nazis were mean to him. He saved my life. He's adorable. He has my heart, for crying out loud. Would a Christian man do anything different?* There were so many reasons he could give that should move the judge, but he wanted to use the right words. And though it sounded strange even to his own ears, he felt like a boy who'd found a hurt puppy and fallen immediately in love with it. Obviously not the most logical thing to say to a judge about a boy. So he was back at the start, unsure how to explain.

"I…uh. Well, he was alone, Your Honor. I couldn't very well leave him in an orphanage run by *Germans,* the very ones who put him in Dachau in the first place. I just couldn't."

Judge Miller leveled a stare in Will's direction. "Boy, all Germans didn't put the little fella there. The Nazis did. There's a huge difference."

Knees about to give out, Will suddenly remembered that Judge Miller was Mrs. Schroeder's brother…their parents had come from Germany. They were both born here. What had possessed him to say such a thing about the Germans. In his heart he knew all of them weren't responsible for the atrocities of war.

"Sorry, Your Honor. I didn't mean to imply—"

"Enough said." The judge held up his palm and then rustled the papers in front of him, steering their conversation back to the matter at hand. Will knew Judge Miller to be a fair man, but he still wished he hadn't spat the word *German* so harshly. *God help my unforgiveness. Change my heart.*

Will looked anywhere but at the judge, but figured the best thing was to jump right back in the game. "Your Honor. You know my family, the support they all will give me. Give us, because Hank and I are in this together. We haven't been apart since he was released, and not because the men in my unit didn't try. They couldn't *pry* Hank's hands off me. And I'll be honest, I didn't want them to. Something happened to me when that little boy grabbed hold of my leg. He gave me a reason for living after the war, a reason to make some good come out of the circumstances. To hope. Mother always taught us that good comes out of every situation if we allow it. And Hank is so much goodness rolled into one little bundle."

"But this simply isn't done, boy," Judge Miller said. "Even if I wanted to, now that you aren't planning to get married, I can't even consider your proposal. Children go to couples, not single men." The judge adjusted his glasses, peering over the top at Will. "You see how inappropriate that would appear."

Will paced the floor of the judge's office. "But you said—"

"I thought you were getting married! I can't change laws, boy. They are what they are."

"Well, then, they're wrong." Will stopped, stared the judge in the eyes. "That boy and I haven't been apart for more than a couple hours at a time. He counts on me for everything. My family is there for him. I'm there for him." He swallowed hard. "And he's there for me. He saved my life. You *have* to let me adopt him, Your Honor." His eyes didn't waver, not one bit. It was imperative he convince the judge. "Just a few seconds ago I was wrong for judging you. Don't judge me for being a single man who wants to adopt. He'll have a huge family to take care of him."

"Don't give me that, William Judge. If I could, I would. I've known you since you were knee high to a porcupine's quills. Shucks, you worked for me summers cataloging cases. I've watched you grow from a clumsy teenager into a rather remarkable young man. You offered yourself up for this country that I love. I know what grit you're made of." He took his glasses off, wiped them with a hankie, and slapped them back on his face. "You don't think I'd move heaven and earth for you to adopt the boy?" Tugging his chin, Miller let out a groan. "Let me talk to the county circuit judge, Harry Peters. See if there's any precedent for this kind of nonsense."

"But, Your Honor."

"William—" he narrowed his gaze "—I said I'll try." He offered a sad excuse for a smile, almost as if he felt guilty about looking happy while Will suffered so. "That's all I can promise. In the meantime you and your folks will keep temporary guardianship. Well, your folks, officially, but we won't hold that technicality over you."

Will nodded and pressed the judge's hand. "I appreciate this, sir. And I can't thank you enough."

Will's mother waited at the door, basket in hand. "I thought you might like to take the boy on a picnic to celebrate." She offered the white wicker basket, smelling of fried chicken, warm bread and chocolate cake.

Will dragged through his teeth the long strand of rye grass he'd picked on the way home. "A bit premature. Judge Miller can't promise anything. You'd think in these tough times the county would be happy to place an orphan where he's wanted, wouldn't you? I live in this country, fought for it, but still don't understand the way the government works, other than the wheels turn slower than spokes in tar. Why do you suppose that is, Mother?"

"Well, I guess they want to be sure. Here's a little boy, thousands of miles from home, barely speaking English. So it would be difficult for him to complain if he weren't being treated right. Yes, I s'pose they just have to be sure he'll be taken care of. And you are young, William. Barely old enough to be a father, and young enough to be a hothead." His mother set down the food and wrapped him in a hug. After all these years, her ample arms still meant safety, assurance that God was in control. "You give the judge a chance to make good on his word. I don't have to tell you he's an honest man, son. If anyone can put that boy in your care, Eric Miller will find the way, don't you think?"

"I only hope you're right. What would I do if—"

"No." She stepped back, grabbed the basket and slipped it into his hands. "Let's not go to thinking dark thoughts, all right? Have faith. You are what is right for that boy. The two of you found each other at a time when you both needed a new start on life, a new reason to live, son. Don't you think?" She reached for a yellow-and-brown afghan, folded it, spread it on top of the basket with gentle but sure hands. When she looked up into his face, she waggled her finger. "God doesn't make mistakes, William. He wouldn't dangle the carrot then give it to another rabbit. This will all work out. Now grab Hank, a baseball glove, and get yourselves on a picnic. Mother's orders."

She always knew exactly what to say. With a mock salute toward her, he let a grin surface. "Yes, ma'am. Will do."

"By the way," she said, eyes glittering with mischief, "I might have packed a tad too much food in the basket. I mean, there're plenty of goodies in there just in case you wanted to take someone else along."

He dropped a kiss on her forehead. "Mother, dear. You are so transparent."

* * *

Abby rewrapped her sister's ankle with another layer of chipped ice, packing the towel firmly around until the entire foot was encased. "Barbara, the swelling is because you're on your feet too much. When the doctor said to stay off, he meant it. I'm here, let me do the work. That's why Mama and Daddy let me stay longer."

Barbara huffed. "Jackson and Grace are my responsibilities."

"And mine. You rest. Keep the foot up."

"Grace is sleeping right now and will be for a while. I'll keep my foot hanging in the air and read a book until all my toes are frozen. Will that work, Nurse Abigail?"

"Very well, only don't get frostbite on those toes."

"Abby, do you have plans? What's there for you to do? Dishes are done, beds are made. I might have another book for you to read. Or better yet, why don't you get out in the fresh air? Go for a walk or something." Her brows wiggled up. "Maybe take Hank out for a while. Strengthen his little legs. I can't believe how strong he's growing. Don't you think he's getting stronger?"

Abby rolled her eyes. "I see right through you, sister dear. Don't be trying to play matchmaker. Poor Will just had his heart broken. The last thing he wants is another female muddying up his life. If truth be known—"

A rap at the door startled both of them. Will opened up and stepped inside. Hank immediately broke from his grasp and dashed to Abby's side. "Abby." Then he giggled, dancing around her. "C'mon, Miss Abby. Wanna play wif us?"

Barbara grinned. "Hmm, what are you going to do, muddy waters?"

Abby lobbed her a wicked glare. Turning to the boy, she asked, "What are you fellows up to this morning?" She tapped on Hank's head with her fingertips, but quickly glanced Will's direction.

He lounged near the doorway, a playful smirk edging his lips and muscles straining the limits of his shirt.

Abby let out a sigh and then looked away, embarrassed he might have seen her ogling him. He grinned and her face grew warmer. "We're going to play a little ball. Thought maybe you and Barbara would like to get out, take the baby for a walk. Then Hank, here, and I could impress you with our amazing ability to hit a baseball."

He was amazing her all right. His military training had left him in such great condition she could barely pry her eyes away. Abby found all she could do was stammer. "Baseball, huh?"

"Yeah. Baseball," Hank mimicked.

Barbara spoke up before Abby could say a word. "My foot's up, like the doctor ordered, and the baby…well, listen. Not a sound of Grace. She's out for a while. Why don't you and Hank take Abby with you? I'm sure the fresh air will do her good. Get her out from under my feet. Like any wonderful little sister, she's smothering me a tad too much."

Abby leveled another glare in Barbara's corner of the room. "But who will take care of you?" *Who will take care of me if I go?* Her heart did weird little things in her chest and the flutters slipped into her stomach. She knew she should stay with Barbara and Grace, let the boys have some time out alone, but Will's lips, thick and firm, had a way of pulling her away from all common sense.

As she openly gawked at him, contemplating those lips, he broke into a smirk that took her breath away. He knew exactly what she was thinking. She should say something or walk away. Just standing here staring discounted every sense of sanity she'd known. "But… Grace might need me. I have to take care of Barbara."

"Not sure I need any taking care of. I've got my book, crutches are close by in case Grace wakes up. My foot is encased in a block of ice. What more could a girl want?" Her look of innocence irritated the socks off Abby. "I'm prepared for any and all situations. Guess you might as well go have some fun and leave me to my *Call of the Wild*."

What an embarrassing situation. If he were interested in Abby, he would have asked her and would not have included Barbara and Grace, right? But he'd asked all of them. That meant he wasn't anxious to give the wrong impression how he felt. If she accompanied them, she'd feel like a third wheel. Two's company, three's a crowd. Barbara had told her that when they were kids. He licked his lips and she blinked. Looking away, her pulse shot up so much she actually felt it thumping in her temples.

Hank looped his hand into hers and tugged. "Please, Miss Abby. You come, too. Be wif us. Wecomome." Staring into those beautiful big eyes, she warmed again, but this time it was Hank who had her heart wrapped around his finger, not Will.

All three laughed, remembering his idea of a greeting, and then Hank chimed in, a big question on his face. "Well, you go wif Hank?"

"Okay." Abby giggled. She could say no to Will and Barbara, but not Hank. He had only to ask and like a royal command, she obeyed. "Let me put together some snacks for us. I have no doubt you'll be hungry before the baseball game is over."

Will strode across the floor in three steps. "Done and done. I come bearing a hearty picnic lunch."

"Grandma Judge pack it," Hank added.

"A basket full of goodies if truth be known." Will lifted the edge of the lid. "I think I smelled fried chicken."

Abby faltered. "Well. Seems she might have known I'd say yes. Am I so transparent your mother packed enough food for three…or more? Fried chicken, huh?"

"And choclit cake." Hank jumped up and down.

Will's brow lifted, daring her to say no to chocolate cake.

Her hand rubbed her tummy as she looked Hank's direction. "You've got me there, buddy." Abby shook her head in resignation. Some things simply couldn't be talked away. Suddenly the feeling that Barbara was playing matchmaker moved behind. Seemed Mrs. Judge was the real matchmaker. "That's not playing fair. You know I can't resist your mother's chocolate cake. How she manages with rationing is beyond me. I'll be so glad when it's completely over." She sighed with the realization that it was useless to fight it. "Let me grab a sweater in case."

When she turned to go, Barbara offered up that irritating smirk one more time. The face that told Abby to take advantage of the circumstances and allow herself the luxury of getting to know Will on a whole different level. Or was that Abby's mind tempting her? Sometimes she couldn't tell the difference.

Out from under the porch's protection headed for the meadow, bright rays of sun beat against their skin. Abby tilted her face up, soaking in the warmth. "This morning is the prettiest yet."

Will turned, nodded with a flash of sass in his eyes. "Very pretty, squirt." Then he clipped her nose as he always did when being impertinent, which was often.

"She a quirt?" Hank wanted to know, inquisitive to each new word.

Will dropped to one knee, set the basket down. "She's a squirt, like you, buddy. I knew Miss Abby when *she* was a little girl. A bratty little girl."

"Bratty?"

Abby's eyes widened, this conversation was quickly deteriorating. "I think Will has it all wrong. *He* was the brat. My sisters and I were perfect young ladies. Never got into trouble while Will liked to pull our hair and tease us."

"Why you tease her, Vill, uh, Will?"

Will stood abruptly and Abby wasn't prepared when he dashed around Hank, grabbed her by the waist, and started tickling her as if she were ten years old again. "Because it's fun, Hank. C'mon and help me."

She felt like a child once more. Then her feet reacted faster than her head and off she ran, Will nipping at her heels.

"Catch 'er, Will. Catch 'er."

Abby, having a second to think, was unsure why

she was running in the first place, but she skimmed across the grassy field. A breeze whisked against her face, blowing her hair in all directions. Will's boots stomped closer and closer. He reached out and missed. She sprinted ahead, but this time, to her delight, he proved quicker. When he grabbed her arm, she spun around and lost her balance. But Will caught her, trapping her in his arms.

Neither said a word; they both just stared, breaths coming in sharp gasps. They had been here before—at this same moment. And now, as if being offered a second chance to get it right, they froze again. If she spoke, the winsome moment would fade. If he spoke, she was afraid of what he might say. *Don't breathe too loudly, Abby.*

Will's eyes didn't look at her, but through her, to another place and time. Germany or their meeting five years ago? She couldn't tell. While the brown of his eyes grew rounder, his hands tightened on her arms. Still not a word. At last he blew out a long breath. Maybe, just maybe in this close proximity, he was thinking of Jeannine.

Chapter 9

Now that he had her, what should he do with her? The moment of tickling her like a child had passed, and he certainly didn't have tickling her on his mind now. Looking at this beautiful woman with hair straggling across her face and down her back, he thought only of kissing her. And that wasn't why he'd asked her along. Was it? Things had become so doggone mixed up where Abby was concerned. What had started out as a nice picnic lunch had deteriorated into his letting his feelings out in a way he didn't like. Opening up through dozens of letters hadn't worked well with Jeannine. What made him think Abby would be any different?

Maybe the look in her eyes that invited him to move closer. That, and this had nothing to do with a stack of letters. Not love letters anyway.

The rest of the world seemed to stop breathing with them as if his decision in the next two seconds would determine the rest of his life. "Abby?" His fingers released her wrist, and his hand traveled over her elbow, up to her shoulder. His other hand closed around the back of her neck and drew her nearer. Nope, nothing to do with letters at all.

"Yes?"

"I'm not sure what I'm going to do, here." This wasn't like pulling her hair or playing a prank on her. He listened as the blood rushed in his head, telling him to act on impulse this one time. It was all right. She wasn't Jeannine and he could trust his gut.

She didn't step away, didn't hint at disliking his nearness. Instead she leaned into his embrace while he fought to control the hammering in his chest. She must be able to hear it.

Again that overpowering feeling that the earth waited for the two of them to turn this corner, make a decision about their futures. He drew in a shaky breath, held it, hoped she would say something to encourage him to explore his feelings further. When she didn't, he let out the air in what became a truly uncomfortable groan. She had to be able to tell he was dying here as he waited for something to happen. Wanting to kiss her, but wary of making a move, he was afraid of hastening the moment away with a wrong word; he remained still—silent.

Her eyes twinkled like tiny stars, bursting with energy. Was that a yes?

In one fluid motion he bent forward, her lips only inches from his. She didn't back away. Her breath feathered over his lips, warming his soul with encouragement. In his imagination he could almost taste her kiss.

Her brow rose ever so slightly asking him if he planned to kiss her or not. *Well? Did he?*

Every noise in the meadow stopped for him. Not a single sound… He took a deep breath and leaned closer yet. "Abby—"

"Will? You gonna play ball?"

No sound but Hank, that is.

They both started at the intrusion and gazed down. Hank had lugged the heavy basket across the field and waited patiently at their feet. "I hungry. We gonna eat or we gonna play ball?"

A sigh escaped Will's lips as his hand slipped from Abby's shoulder. He glanced at the upturned face and chuckled. "Yes, buddy. We can eat first and then play ball." He grinned at Abby, a shake of his head apologizing for the interruption. So close. They had almost had the chance to explore their feelings, try each other on for size. But right now, right here, Hank's needs came first.

Abby dropped to Hank's side. "You want to play ball or have lunch first?"

"Play ball. Play ball. Have fun!"

Will stared over the boy's head, his gaze coming to rest on Abby's lips. "I was planning a bit of fun myself, buddy. But I think it's a good idea we're gonna play ball."

With the lightest touch, Abby placed a hand on Will's arm. "Probably better for him to play and then eat anyway. Won't upset his tummy as much."

He should have thought of that. Being a dad wasn't as easy as his father made it seem. Maybe he'd been a smidge preoccupied. Something he'd have to think on in the future.

Abby grabbed some bright wildflowers and paced off a small diamond, then placed the blooms around as bases while Will showed Hank how to hold a bat. With all the patience he could muster, he slipped Hank's hands around the base of it, helping him grip it as tightly as possible. Then he allowed him a couple of careful swings over the wild daisy plate. On the first slice through the air, Hank swung completely around, the weight of the bat carrying him. But over and over he swung until he was able to hoist it to knee level with some dexterity.

Abby grabbed the ball and strode to the pitcher's mound, winding up, showing off what a tomboy she was at heart. The game would be Hank against Will. Since Abby played umpire as well as pitcher, Will already knew who would win this game. Her face gave away the winner before they even started.

Hank ran all the bases, each hit, with Will pretending to fall, slowing just in time for Hank to get another home run. Abby laughed until tears trickled over her cheeks. They soon had a tired but hungry boy anxious for fried chicken and homemade bread with butter.

After the last wedge of chocolate cake disappeared, Will and Abby sat on the blanket watching Hank, with his second wind, throw the ball as far as he could and run around the bases. He didn't seem to tire of throwing, running and retrieving the ball to start all over again.

"He's putting some well-deserved baby fat on those bones," Abby said.

Will hadn't realized how much until her comment. "I guess he is. No more spindly legs like a foal. Yes, you're right." He glanced her way. "Mother's chocolate cake doesn't hurt when it comes to fattening up little boys. I was her first project. Jackson lucked out. Never did like sweets all that much." He patted his stomach. "But me? I always begged and whined for more. If it hadn't been for the peanuts, I would have lived on sugar. I guess they helped more than hurt."

Abby eyed him rather brazenly for a second. "Sweets didn't seem to harm you any."

"I think boot camp helped me more than lack of sweets. They have a way of turning boys into men. Or something like that."

Her gaze slid over him one more time causing him to suck back air. Then she picked a dandelion and tossed it at him, turning their moment playful again. "I'm the one all the cookies and cakes hurt," she said. "Nothing is going to fit when I return home."

His eyes raked over her and she shivered, though the sun was warmer than before. He seemed to be taking in every inch of her figure. "No, you're perfect just the way you are."

A breath hitched in her throat and she didn't know how to respond. "Now, you're teasing me again. Shame on you, Will Judge. Like always. You love to tease."

"No, Abby. I'm not sure why I didn't see it a long time ago. I'd been thinking of you as the freckle-faced kid. Even when your letters came, my only image of you was with pigtails down to your shoulders and a turned-up nose." He held her chin with his thumb and forefinger and did that funny inspection of her again that left her breathless. "Now you're anything but a gangly kid. Though you do still have that cute little turned-up nose."

The blush started at her neck and worked its way

up and down her body until the warmth covered her like a thick quilt on a winter night. "You've changed, too, Will."

He grinned. "Taller, huh?"

Finally she relaxed. "Yes, a lot taller. And other things."

He crept closer on the blanket. "So, tell me. What other things about me have you all worked up?"

The coziness she'd felt turned into full-blown mortification. He was mind reading again. She tugged her chin back. "You are quite full of yourself, Mr. Judge. I don't remember saying I was all worked up. You have me confused with all your other girls."

He tugged the curl on her neck, his fingers brushing the tender skin under her ear. *Stop, Will, before I wrap my arms around you.*

"Abby, darlin', I'd never confuse you with anyone else. Not even with one of my dozens of beautiful girls."

She quivered against his fingertips. And the look in his eyes led her to believe he'd read every emotion in that action. How could he, in such a short time, know her so well? But he did. Any other time with any other man she would have bolted. Or given him what for. Will was different. His soul called out to hers and left her all the more anxious to dig deeper into his thoughts, into his dreams and goals. She longed to know every curve of his face. Her gaze skittered over his eyes, his nose, and came to rest on his mouth. Then she shuddered and looked away. Too much daydreaming. Too personal.

And yet she didn't move as Will edged closer.

Abby swallowed the lump in her throat, withered

under his scrutiny, and realizing what he was about to do, closed her eyes.

His lips touched hers, just for a moment. Sweetness and a tenderness she'd never imagined swelled her heart. Well, this was what she'd wanted. No way would she stop him now. Nothing could stop him.

"Will? Do you see me? Do you see me?" Hank hollered.

Will's laughter brushed her lips a second time. "I see you. I see you," he called back with a groan. He touched the end of Abby's nose and grinned. "I guess I'm not supposed to do that. Didn't realize we had our own little chaperone along to protect you from my wicked ways." He lifted his brows dramatically.

Heart pounding, Abby said, "Maybe you're right. We should head back. At least see what Hank's up to." She sighed, the rush of air breaking a surreal feeling that had trapped her.

Will squinted at Hank. "I wondered if his legs would ever be strong enough to run again. Never know what starvation does to the body. And look at him now."

She couldn't help it, the comment brought tears to her eyes. "How could they, Will? A child. A little child who could no more hurt them than, oh, I can't believe what they did."

His arm lifted, came to rest around her shoulder. Then he pulled her head to his chest and spoke soothing words. "This was war, Abby. Men do things they would never even think of doing at any other time. I'm not defending them, especially not for genocide. I hate what they did to so many innocent people, but war is war. There is nothing nice about it. Not even the outcome. Because sooner or later the hatred derived from this end will only incite another round of killing. Another round of grabbing what one country can get from another." As his hand stroked her hair, she was ten again and her father talked to her ever so gently explaining how cruel people could be. "How can I expect you to understand, when I don't understand and I was there?"

He was right, of course. Women gave birth to the baby boys who went to war; men ordered the war. How could a woman ever be expected to see it the same way? If anyone ever hurt one of her babies, well, she'd have plenty to say on the subject. She pulled back, looked up. "Will, you're so forgiving. How can you?" *I'm having trouble forgiving what happened to Hank and I wasn't there to see the horrors.*

"Hating only hurts the person who hates, Abby. Not the other way around. When this war is over, we'll have to find a way to get past our feelings. To try and accept each other again, move forward. After the Great War, we all got along again, for a while. Then money was scarce and Hitler looked for someone to blame. He found them. The same people who have been blamed for centuries."

She patted his chest, allowing the muscles under her hand to offer a semblance of safety over her thoughts. "You're such a hero, Will. You and the men who served."

"The people who helped the Jews escape are the real heroes. You'll see. One day we'll know all about them. Stories are already slipping out about folks who gave up their homes to help escapees. They're the true heroes of this war. People like Hank's parents. When he's old enough, we'll find out all we can about them. Somehow."

"You sound so much like Daddy. I mean," she stammered as the blush covered her cheeks again, "not old, like Dad, but your thoughtfulness is a lot like his. He's always looking for the good in people. And he forgives so easily, like you. I like knowing you, William Judge."

He tipped up her chin with his fingers. "And I like knowing you." A deep sigh slipped from his lips as he looked around. He held her shoulders and his fingers squeezed—hard. Was he remembering?

She thought she understood. He'd said too much; his feelings were still all mixed together. The chore fell to her to keep their minds on track. "I think we'd better clean up here and head back with Hank. He's going to need a nap after all the running around."

Will nodded. "You're right, of course. I have to learn to think of those things if I'm going to do a good job as a father."

Abby realized that Hank was foremost in Will's thoughts. And for good reason. The boy needed him. "You'll do wonderfully. I'm sure of it." *That's right. Keep it friendly, nothing more. After all, in spite of what had happened here today, he's probably still in love with Jeannine.* "And I need to get back and help Barbara."

Chapter 10

Ear-piercing screams ricocheted off the bedroom walls, hauling Will from peaceful sleep. He jumped from his bed, flipped on the light on the nightstand and did a hasty inspection of the boy. Nothing physically wrong, so he pulled Hank to his chest. Hank slugged him in the face. Then kicked his legs against Will's thighs.

"No! Zostaw mnie w spokoju!" Hank shoved at Will's chest, clawed at his face with incredible strength for such a small boy.

"Buddy, it's me, it's Will." He pinned Hank's arms to his sides, but the boy's eyes didn't open and he kept screaming the same phrase over and over. Will witnessed the absolute terror on Hank's face. After a few more seconds of attacks he began to quiet, tears streaming out of his eyes.

"No! Mamuszia! Mamuszia!" Finally his lids lifted

and he focused on Will's face. "Vill?" he cried, slipping back into his strong accent. "Dat'chou?"

"Yeah, it's me, buddy." He tugged Hank closer and stroked the soft, bristly hair. "You okay?"

"I have bad dream. Very bad." He swiped his eyes with the back of his hand. "You get Mamuszia?"

Will's mind raced. "Mamu-what?"

"Me mamuszia?" His eyes, hopeful for a second, suddenly refilled with tears of reality. His body slumped in Will's arms. With all the fight gone, he resigned himself to the reality of the moment. "No, she gone, right, Vill? My mama gone?"

Like a slug in the gut, his words ripped into Will's heart. He finally understood the depth of being a parent. How painful it was to see a child suffer. Hank understood she was gone, but in the same vein, he couldn't put the thoughts in their proper places. *Why, Lord?* "She's gone, buddy. I'm sorry. But I'm here. Can I help you?"

Hank's head dropped against his chest. "No. The monsters, they don't leave me alone when I sleep."

"What monsters, Hank?"

"Bad men with dogs. They scare children. I say, 'Leave me alone,' but they keep come at me." His little hands clamped onto Will's arms as if hanging on for dear life. "You don't leave Hank alone, right V—Will. You help me?" The fingers dug into Will's muscles, hard enough he lessened the grip.

"I can try and help, buddy. Want me to rub your back until you fall asleep?"

His head shook vehemently. After a second his eyes lit. "You get Miss Abby? She come?"

"Would you like that?"

"Yes. She sleep with me?"

"Miss Abby's at Gracie's, buddy." Hank looked toward the door as if she might miraculously materialize. At least he obviously hoped she would.

"You sit here, all right? I'll go call her."

"Call her? Now?" Hope etched his features again. This was something Will *could* do to help. "Dziekuje." He buried his face in Will's chest and continued to clutch his pajama top. Sobs filtered through the cloth and rested heavily on Will's ears. How he hated for Hank to hurt. Then Will heard the one word he had come to understand. It continued like a chant from the frightened face. "Dziekuje. Dziekuje." Hank was always thanking him for something, so grateful for the smallest crumbs at his table.

Will kissed the creased forehead. "You're welcome, buddy." Will wrapped the quilt around his shoulders—tightly, like swaddling a baby.

Jackson had insisted on driving Abby around to the next road rather than allow her to run across the properties between the houses. "Thanks, Jackson. I'll be back in the morning." She hoisted her small bag and sprinted for the porch where Will waited with the door open. This had to be serious.

He hurried her through the front room. "I'm really sorry to be a bother, but he woke up screaming. Bad dreams about the soldiers, he said. He's only starting to talk about them. I guess it's hard to find the right words in English, but if you could have seen the terror in his eyes. He didn't need words to explain how horrifying

Dachau was for adults, let alone a small boy. Just how big a threat did the soldiers think he was, anyway?"

"Oh, Will. Where is he?"

"First I bundled him up in the quilt from the bed until he calmed down a bit. Then I poured him some milk and dug out a couple of cookies. It's all I know to do, just like Mother used to do to scare the monsters away when I was Hank's age, soothe the tummy."

Abby rushed into the parlor, where Hank sat before a crackling fire, shivering. Will had replaced the heavy quilt with a small blanket. Hank held the cup of milk with both hands. The cup trembled. The cookies went untouched. His eyes, glassy and fixed, stared at the flames in the fireplace.

Abby drew closer without hesitation. "You okay, Hank?" she whispered.

He dropped the empty cup on the rug and dove toward her, the blanket slipping to the floor. His arms immediately wrapped around her legs like they were a lifeline. "Miss Abby. I dreameded. They no give me bread. Other boy take it away and they no give me more. I so hungry, Miss Abby. And the soldiers, they—"

"Shh." She sank to the floor, slid Hank into her arms and kissed the tears from his cheeks. "You aren't going to be hungry again, Hank. I promise you that. I can't explain how I know, I just do. And we won't let those bad men ever come near you." She looked up at Will, her line of vision drawing Hank's the same direction. "Will won't let them hurt you anymore. Will's very strong and likes to protect the people he loves. And he loves you very much."

"Dziekuje." His forehead furrowed. "Sorry. I say tank you. Dat right?"

She mopped the rest of the tears with the sleeve of her sweater, but moisture stuck in his long, sooty lashes. "You can say whatever makes you feel better, little man. I love you, Hank." Then she let go of him long enough to hold her arms out wide like her mother used to. "I love you this much."

His scrawny arms opened wide and the hint of a smile broke through the clouds. "Miss Abby, ja cie kocham. Dat mean I love you, Miss Abby." He stretched wide again. "Dis much, I loves you."

A sob choked Will and he had to step from the room. To let a child starve. A child who was just a toddler at the time. How could they? And Hank had told him they slapped him when he asked for food. He leaned back with his head against the wall, drew in a deep breath and tried to calm his nerves. Certain lines should never be crossed. The soldiers could hurt *him* and fighters like him—that was war. They could hurt adults who understood they were fighting, but a child? His hands curled into fists at his sides as he did his best to remember what he'd told Abby. They had to move forward, learn to forgive. It was one thing to lecture someone else about forgiveness, another thing entirely to do it yourself. *How is that possible, God? How can I forgive grown men who would hurt a child? A man's son? My son...*

Even as he thought about a son dying, he realized God understood well enough. He had waited while men killed His son for no reason other than jealousy. And the more Will thought about it, wars were fought for the same reason. One nation jealous of another.

His gut clenched as a groan hissed from his chest. War didn't solve a thing. And yet men fought year after year, decade after decade, century after century. For what? To extend a boundary a few miles? To capture prisoners?

He envisioned Jackson's burns from the bombing at Pearl Harbor. How Jack had suffered, thinking people would be frightened of his appearance. Of how the family had fought with him to show up at his sister's wedding. Then wonderful Barbara had taught him what love was all about. Jackson *had* moved on. Had forgiven. Now it was Will's turn.

Somehow it felt different when a child suffered the painful repercussions of war. But he couldn't raise Hank to believe in God's ability to forgive if Will didn't believe it himself. *God, my strength will have to come from You. I guess I'm not that forgiving a person after all. And I want to be able to teach Hank in truth.*

Soft footsteps on the stairs drew him into the hallway. A flick of the light switch forced the darkness away, for now. A head full of cloth curls met him. His mother.

"Is Hank all right?" Her anxious face squeezed sleep away.

Will patted her hand—cold. With worry, no doubt. "He's fine. You go back to sleep. Hank asked for Abby and she's here now."

"If you need anything…"

An hour later, after Abby had coaxed Hank to eat the cookies and Mother had been convinced to return to her room, Will and Abby settled Hank into his bed.

Will gave up his own bed to Abby and went to sleep in Betty's old bedroom. The faint lyrics of "Twinkle, Twinkle, Little Star" followed his footsteps down the hall. He pictured them both, arms around each other, Hank's head on Abby's shoulder, his tears dry at last.

The house was as it should be again, at peace. Only the gong of the clock in the parlor each hour broke the silence. But Will found it difficult to nod off as he imagined a little boy only a month ago fighting sleep, hungry and cold.

And afraid.

Chapter 11

The next day between yawns, Will drove to the train station to pick up his sister, Bets, and her husband, Teddy. They'd been gone longer than planned because of Ted's father. At first there wasn't much hope his father would survive the heart attack, but Mrs. Barrymore didn't give up, and now Ted's father had rallied.

Leaping from the train through the haze of steam, Betty drew Will into a bear hug. "Mother told me about Hank. Are you really going to adopt him? Oh, Will. How wonderful! I always said you would make a wonderful father one day."

Will chuckled. "How's that?"

"Because you've never really grown up." She eyed him closely. "But you have, haven't you? The war has made a man of you. Whether you wanted to become one or not. Oh, Will. Both you and Jackson had to go fight. I'm so sorry. But look at you now."

His arms opened wide. "Had to happen eventually." Then he tweaked her nose and laughed. He didn't want to get into another depressing talk about war. "As for adopting Hank, I'm trying. Now that Jeannine and I aren't getting married, the red tape's grown longer and brighter. Judge Miller is doing all he can to find out if it's possible. But if you'll keep us in prayer, we'll see what we see."

His sister pecked his cheek. "You know you'll have plenty of good character references to go along with a slightly eccentric family. And Mother and Daddy are so excited."

"They are?"

"Of course, silly. You think they wouldn't be?"

His fingers reached up, like always, rifling through what used to be long hair. "Hard to tell sometimes. We haven't really talked through it much. I'm certain they like Hank, but they act like I've bitten off more than I can chew."

"Well, haven't you, little brother?" Betty turned as Teddy jumped down.

The telltale sheepish grin tugged at the corners of Will's mouth. Same as always when his big sis backed him into the corner. "Yeah, maybe I have. But this is one big bite I'm glad about. One I know I'll be able to follow through. Not like the paper route that you and Jackson had to finish for me."

What a bum he'd been at fourteen. He liked to refer to those as his bum years. Always starting projects but never completing them. About time he grew up.

Betty smiled and tugged Teddy's arm. "Could you grab the rest of our bags, sweetie?" When she spun back and clutched Will, she said, "Oh, Will, I've missed you. I'm so happy you're home. And I can't wait to meet Hank. This makes me an auntie twice over, doesn't it? I have a new nephew *and* niece. Twice blessed."

Will laughed when he saw all the luggage Betty had taken with them. Figured he'd better help Teddy or they'd be at the station all day long. Some things didn't change even with the passage of time and events. The conductor hollered over the noise at the station as they loaded the car.

Once the train pulled away again, Will drove across the tracks and whisked them to the house where Mother had dinner warming in the oven.

The reunion dinner lasted longer than he'd planned, but not so late he couldn't surprise Hank. After overwhelming the little guy with the new relatives, Will thought it best to do an activity with him—alone. *Just us guys* he explained to Hank, who shouted and clapped his hands. "Us guys. Us guys. Us guys. Vussat mean?"

"It means we're going to see a special showing of *Snow White* at the movies."

"A snow girl?"

Will held his hand a couple inches below Hank's head. "And seven tiny men. One, two, three, four, five, six, seven." Then he gave Hank a noogie. "You'll see. Now go ask Grandma Judge to help you put your shoes on."

"She not a grandma. She a babunia. She be *my* babunia?"

Will dropped on one knee. "Do you want her to be?"

The arms he'd grown so comfortable with squeezed his neck. "Yes, Will."

"Then go ask her. I think she might like that."

Face washed, shoes on and in a spiffy new jacket, Hank walked with Will into the theatre. Will realized how much he had wanted to ask Abby to go along, but the need for Hank to have time alone with him took precedence. He was sure she understood. Hank's ability to trust him was crucial if the adoption were to go through as planned.

Hank danced back and forth, trying to see over the heads of the people waiting in line. Will smiled, remembering how difficult it was as a youngster to wait patiently. Finally, tickets in hand, Will and Hank stepped to the concession stand. Hank's eyes grew wide as he took in all the candy. "Vill?"

Will dropped to Hank's level again, something he caught himself doing many times each day. "Wuh. Wuh, Will," he said. The little fella slipped into his natural speech patterns the more tired he became. But Will would continue to remind him.

"Okay. Wuh-wuh, Will." Hank giggled and pointed to a box of bright colors.

"Good choice." He stood and ordered. "Popcorn and Jujubes, please."

"Jubes?"

"Close enough, pardner." Will put the candy in his pocket, then balancing the popcorn in one hand, he held Hank's with the other.

In the lobby a family of children lined up, danced

around them, and sang the dwarves' songs. He chuck-led when Hank tried to mimic, doing his best "hi ho."

"Willie, is that you?"

He heard the voice and shriveled inside. Like one of Hank's nightmares come back to haunt him, Jeannine appeared as if out of nowhere. And while a lump filled his throat, her voice grated like stones tumbling over one another. He had managed the past few days to avoid her, even in their small town. But at present there didn't seem to be an escape.

Turning, he watched as she bent low, welcoming a beaming Hank into her arms. "Miss Jeannine. Hi." Hank glanced up at Will. "Hi ho." He giggled.

"Oh, look there, you little cutie. Buttered popcorn and everything. Would you boys mind if I sat with you? I'm here all by myself. And watching a movie by one-self isn't very much fun, now is it?" She flashed her best smile. "I've missed you, Hank. And you…Will."

"Okay, W-Will?" Hank's ability to love when getting nothing in return amazed Will. But he wasn't fooled. Jeannine was up to no good. And what was with the batting eyes? Seemed like she'd already seen too many movies. He couldn't very well disappoint Hank or em-barrass Jeannine in the middle of the theater lobby. He didn't wish her ill will, but he also didn't want her around Hank. Or him, if he were honest with himself. If she stayed in New Hope, he would have no choice but to run into her on occasion. However, he would keep the meetings brief and to the point.

He still kicked himself for ever asking her out in the first place. Men. They tended to think with their eyes. They just assumed that a beautiful girl must be beautiful inside as well. But he'd learned the hard way that wasn't necessarily so.

In spite of her imposing on their day, the movie went very well once they strolled inside. Hank enjoyed himself and Jeannine proved pleasant enough company, but he didn't want her getting the wrong idea. Before they left he would be clear about where he stood in case his and Hank's jackets on the seat between them wasn't hint enough.

As they were leaving the theater, he twisted in her direction. "Thank you for being so kind to Hank. I'm sure we'll see you around town from time to time."

Her pout followed his steps louder than words. When he turned he saw the hurt on her face and guilt sneaked past his anger. They wouldn't do this again; it sent the wrong message to even hint that they might get back together.

Jeannine's expression, on the other hand, made it clear she would get what she wanted—even if it meant using Hank to her advantage.

The boys walked in the door, singing "hi ho, hi ho" like the seven dwarfs. When they entered the parlor, Abby pulled Hank onto her lap and peeked in his mouth. "I see you had Jujubes."

"How you know, Miss Abby?"

"Well, you have all different colors stuck in your teeth."

"Yup." He smacked his mouth. "You right. Still taste like red."

"Well, we shall have to brush your teeth before bed."

He giggled and wrapped his arms around her neck. "Miss Jeannine like Jubes, too."

Her supper revisited her throat with an angry bite, but she managed a smile for Hank while swallowing the burn. "That's nice. Did she go to the movies with you?"

"Uh-huh."

Well, she'd thought they were finished. Apparently not. And he could take Jeannine or anyone else to the movies if he wanted. Abby didn't have any particular claim on Will *or* Hank for that matter. A wrenching breath hitched inside her. That might be, but if that were the case, she wouldn't allow herself to grow any closer to them. She had a right to protect her heart. After tonight she would stop coming to stay with Hank. It wasn't smart to let him think of her as he might a mother. Not smart at all.

With determined steps Will landed by her side and helped her to her feet. He draped an arm over her shoulder and leaned close. "We ran into her," he whispered, his voice low and husky. "She invited herself and I didn't want to make a scene in front of Hank. I figured that sent a bad message about manners."

She shrugged out of his hold. "And why should I care one way or the other?"

"I don't know." He smirked and pecked her cheek. "But I think maybe you do."

Abby stepped under his arm and retraced her steps to stand next to Hank. "Shall we get you ready for bed? You have a lot of butter on your mouth. Maybe a bath is in order."

Will peered at her from the corner of his eyes as he rounded the corner for the kitchen.

Hank bit the edge of his lip, obviously deep in thought for a four-year-old. "You sleep here, Miss Abby?"

"I suppose I could. Barbara's much better now. If I stayed again, would that help you not to have nightmares?" At Will's grin all her good intentions took flight.

"I tink so. I like to have Mamuszia near."

"Mamuszia?"

"Mama. You like Mama. You smell nice and hug nice and you always singing. Mamuszia sing to me at night. And she scare away monsters. Yup, you Mamuszia. I remember her now."

As much as she longed to be part of the *Will and Hank* family, Abby recognized this wasn't her choice. She couldn't allow Hank to accept her as a mother figure. So she drew him close and did her best to explain. "Hank, I love you so much, but I'm not your mama. You'll always have her here."

Without warning he looked around the room. "Where?"

She pointed to his chest. "In your heart."

"Like da Jesus man?"

"Will told you about Him?"

"Yup. Say He live in my heart." His face brightened. "With Mama."

"You must have a very big heart. Lots of room for all the people you love." She smiled her best, longing to bring him comfort.

"Yes, Miss Abby. Da biggest room for you and Will. I love you."

He spiked out of her grasp and ran up the stairs. "Go for baf!" The tender moment of introspection vanished as Hank sprinted up the stairs. How quickly a child moved on with his life. She'd like that ability. Then maybe hearing about Will being with Jeannine wouldn't hurt so much.

"I'm coming."

Will's steps sounded louder on the floor as he came from the kitchen. "Abby." Coming to rest next to her, he touched her elbow, sending all kinds of flutters through her stomach. "I didn't ask Jeannine to the movies. Please believe me. She invited herself—and in front of the boy. I would have asked you, but I wanted time alone with Hank. While that didn't work out particularly well, my intentions were good. Next time I won't be that foolish. And I won't think of not asking you. You are the only person I want with me."

Warmth squiggled through her, but she couldn't allow him to see what he did to her unless she knew for sure that he and Jeannine truly had called it quits. She brushed his hand from her arm. "What makes you think I want there to be a next time?"

Chapter 12

Sooner than he would have liked, Will had no choice but to return to work full days as the manager. His father needed his help. His body hadn't fully recovered and his duties as mayor kept him busy enough. Jackson helped less and less as he built up his carpentry shop. Fortunately Will hadn't run into Jeannine again, and she hadn't been so bold as to call. But Abby kept her distance nonetheless, spending less and less time at his folks' and more time with Barbara and Grace. Though, to her credit, she invited Hank along with her on most of their outdoor excursions.

He would have to discuss Hank's care with his mother. Would she want to start raising another little boy? Maybe Will should look for a place of his own and a woman to come in and care for Hank. So many issues to sort out in such a short period of time. Today Hank had cried when Will dressed for work.

"But Miss Abby, she wif Gracie. She go wif Aunt Barbara to doctor."

"You have Grandma Judge to stay with you," Will said. "Won't it be fun to bake cookies with her?"

Hank's head listed to the side. "Okay. It fun to bake cookies. But I miss you, Will. You be home for lunch?"

"I'll be home."

Will twisted aside to put his boots on, his mind rummaging through the many changes he'd initiated at the factory: new work hours, better chances for advancement, the new and improved packaging set up for orders, and most importantly, the opportunity for the workers to miss time for *being in the family way*. And it seemed as if a lot of them had gotten in the family way since many of the men had returned home. The idea of the women continuing to work intrigued him. Why? What would make them put their families on hold now that their men were back? Some of the men.

There were a lot of things to be squared away, and then he'd be home for lunch.

Hank scampered out of their room, no doubt looking for Grandma. He returned and peeked around the corner. Finger in the air, he said, "I come find you, bring you home for lunch together."

For the second time Will rattled off the mental list of *to dos* once he hit his office this morning. Time had proved to be his enemy the past few days, but the work had to be completed if he wanted the new factory procedures up and running. Hank said something to him. Will glanced over. "What? Oh, okay. Sure, buddy. I'll get my work done and we'll have lunch together."

* * *

Just as planned, the doctor's visit had gone well. Barbara's ankle was healing nicely, and Abby brought her back to the Judges' in time for lunch. Mrs. Judge had offered to fix leftover ham and sweet potatoes for them. Abby couldn't wait to sink her teeth into those delicious potatoes as well as the spicy applesauce loaded with honey that Mrs. Judge had her stirring to accompany the meat. Barbara lounged in the chair nearest the back window while lunch warmed in the oven.

Abby scanned the kitchen, expecting Hank to run in any minute. It wasn't like him to miss a meal. From the first time she'd laid eyes on him, his tummy had ruled his behavior, and good thing, too, because he'd needed meat on those bones. She hardly remembered how he'd looked the day he'd arrived at the train station. The only image that entered her mind was skin stretched over bones, but no longer. Now he even had the start of a small tummy, encouraged by lots of cookies and milk. And surprisingly they didn't seem to spoil his dinner—ever.

She turned from the stove. "Mrs. Judge? Did Hank go outside to play?" By now the smells had usually lured him in.

"Just as soon as I said I was fixing lunch. It's good to see he isn't afraid he won't be fed anymore. He grabbed his truck and out the door he went."

Abby listened; no sound from the front of the house. "I didn't notice him on the porch when we came in." Her stomach tumbled a time or two. "Maybe I should go check. He's probably hiding in the flower bushes again. Or playing in the backyard." Letting the spoon sit against the side of the pan, she turned down the heat and wiped her hands on a dishtowel then hurried from the kitchen.

Mrs. Judge continued slicing the ham. "Tell him time to wash up, all right? Lunch in five minutes. Oh, and see if you can spot Will coming over the road. He said he'd be here."

"Certainly."

Abby stepped outside. On the porch she leaned over the railing, checked the rain barrel to be sure no little feet stuck out—a fear of every homeowner—then turned to the bushes. "Hank, time for lunch. Hank!"

A rustle in the rose bush drew her attention, and she breathed a sigh. Finally he'd come out of hiding. Will would have to broach the subject with Hank. They couldn't have him hiding in the bushes and scaring the family half to death. "Come on out, Hank."

But a second later Tawny, the neighbor's tabby, crawled under the lowest branch and rubbed her face against the leaves. Not Hank, but a cat.

"Hank, it's lunch." This time she put elbow grease into the call. "Come in now. Hank, no hiding. Grandma Judge has lunch all ready."

She drew in a calming breath and trudged to the back of the house. The door to the woodshed swung open and closed again. No doubt the little rascal was hiding now that he'd heard her calling him to come in. She'd walk around the corner and out would jump the Hank-in-the-box. He loved to surprise her. Pretend to scare her from his hidey places.

"Hank. Come out of there. Grandma has lunch on the table."

She rounded the corner of the shed, looked into an empty building and a pent-up breath whooshed from her throat. If not there, then where?

With acre upon acre to be searched, Abby set off across the back of the property to inspect each of his favorite hiding places.

First Will heard the clock gong twelve, then he glanced out the window behind his desk and noticed Abby running full out along the side of the road. What was she doing in front of the factory? Maybe Mother had sent his lunch here today. And good thing, he was hungry as a bear.

He stepped out of the office to the front door. "Abby?" No lunch pail. "Where are you headed in such a hurry?"

She dove at him, clutching his arm. "Hank's missing."

"Missing?"

"He isn't at the house. We can't find him. The last your mother saw him, he was headed to the front porch with his truck. I thought maybe he'd come here."

"I'm sure he's just—"

"No! Will, I searched the entire piece of property behind your folks' house. I went as far as Barbara and Jackson's, Betty and Ted's. I even crawled under all the bushes in front of the house. He isn't there, I'm telling you."

Fearful notions swirled through his head, but now wasn't the time for foolish worry. "Where could he have gone? He wouldn't leave with a stranger. I've managed to get that much across to him—not that he would after his experiences with the soldiers. And he wouldn't wander away. Would he?"

Will stopped short, the morning conversation repeating in his head. "He said he'd see me for lunch."

"What does that mean?"

"Just a minute." His thoughts tumbled as he tried to focus on Hank's exact words. "Oh, no."

"What?" Abby's hands tightened on his arm. "Will, what are you thinking?"

"He didn't say he'd meet me for lunch, he said he'd come *get* me for lunch. Oh, Abby, he planned to walk to the factory. C'mon. We can't waste time talking."

He shouted orders to his floor manager and closed the door behind him. "Let's retrace your steps, the way he would have come." He clutched her to him, practically dragging her off her feet.

"I crossed Main. Same as always and I didn't see any sign of him."

Will stopped and chewed the edge of his lip until it hurt. "Then we'll go back the west side. Across to Main instead of straight through. It's the only other way he might know."

Pulling Abby by the arm once again, Will ran as fast as the two could go. They dashed over the path and into town across the end of their street. Abby stopped suddenly, yanking on Will's arm. He spun around. "What?"

"Here. Look, Will."

He stumbled to her side, his insides jolting at the sight. Hank's truck, half hidden in the lilac bushes at the corner of Main and Maple where Hank liked to play when they were shopping in town. Will dashed into Mr.

Perkins's store. "You seen Hank out here? He wandered off and his truck's outside under the lilacs."

"Can't say as I have seen him, Will. Your little guy, right?"

"Yes, Hank."

"Nope. Not today, anyhow. Say, how about you and your folks—"

Will sprinted out the door again, not caring about anyone's feelings but Hank's. What if he'd wandered too far off and was lost? Couldn't find his way back? He'd be afraid again, and the thought of Hank ever having to feel scared sent his mind reeling. He grabbed Abby's hand and tucked it around his elbow again. "Let's go back to the factory, look around once more and I'll call home from there. Someone *has* to have seen him. New Hope isn't exactly Chattanooga. Not a lot of places to get lost."

They barreled toward the factory, sides heaving, and eyes darting, taking in every spot a little boy might hide in. "Hank! Come on, son. Time to go home for lunch!"

Abby shouted as loud or louder than Will, surprising him. There was no doubt in his mind how she felt about Hank. "Come on. We can't stand around waiting for him to show up."

He cupped his hands to his mouth. "Hank!"

Outside the front door of the factory, they discovered him at last. Jeannine held him by the hand. Will looked first at Jeannine and Hank and then back at Abby. Anger surged through Will, but he knew better than to speak until he thought this through. *Count to ten. At least.* He'd have to rely on more than mottos to calm down.

Yelling and scrambling out of Jeannine's grasp, Hank

tripped over his feet to get to Will. "We get ice cream, Will. Choclit."

"You what?" Will glanced in Jeannine's direction. "You took Hank for ice cream?"

She slipped her weight to one hip and eyed him with a catlike expression. "I saw him wandering around by himself and assumed someone," she lingered over the word and gazed at Abby, "was busy doing heaven knows what instead of watching him like she was supposed to. She must have lost him. I figured the best thing to do so he wouldn't be frightened was to buy him some ice cream and then walk him home." She toyed with the purse on her arm. "I guess I was right, now, wasn't I? And here he is, none the worse for wear. Just a touch of chocolate above his lip." Her hip jutted to the side while she fingered the clasp on her bag. She rolled her eyes at Abby.

Will kept his anger in check, but the way his pulse raced, he didn't trust the words that might come out of his mouth. He directed his attention to Abby, speaking softly. "Maybe you should take Hank inside and get him cleaned up. There are towels in my locker. Call Mother, if you don't mind. I'm sure she's beside herself." He glared at Jeannine. "You and I should talk."

Abby led the boy by the hand as he waved fingers over his shoulder. "Tank you, Miss Jeannine. Ice cream good."

Once Hank and Abby stepped inside the building, Will turned to Jeannine. "I don't know what little game you're playing, but don't make Hank part of this. Our relationship is over, Jeannine. He shouldn't have been with you."

"*You* made Hank part of it when you brought him home, Will. We were supposed to get married this summer. You promised me. And look where that got us. All because you wanted to play protector to a boy you aren't even related to. He should be home in Germany or Poland or wherever his people are."

"Jeannine, you had no right to take Hank."

"I *found* Hank. I didn't take him. You should get a better babysitter before you go accusing me of anything, William Judge. Or maybe you should keep closer watch on your girlfriend. Where was she, I ask you? She must have been busy elsewhere when she should have been seeing to Hank."

Will longed to grab her and shake her until her teeth rattled inside her head, but his father had raised him better than that. Drawing in a deep breath, he waited to stop his body from shaking. *Leave it alone, Will. Don't be part of her game. Just leave it alone.*

He straightened and took two steps back, enough distance to be heard without the temptation of throttling her. He strongly suspected she'd taken Hank from the front yard by promising him ice cream. He drew in a cleansing breath to regain his composure. And then again, maybe not. She might have found him on the way to the factory and simply decided to make an opportune moment out of it. No matter the circumstances, he should be considerate. "Thank you for finding him, Jeannine. We all appreciate that you took the time to help him."

"You know I'll always help. After all, someone has to. It's quite obvious you can't trust the people whose care you've put him in. That girl should be taken to task." She swirled her long red hair over her shoulder in a defiant posture. "You should talk to her, Will. People should get what they deserve."

Count to ten and way beyond. She isn't worth it. "Here, Jeannine, since you feel that way." He pulled his hand from his pocket and pitched a quarter her direction. "This should cover the ice cream. And by the way, I'll let my *mother* know you don't care for her babysitting skills."

Her face fell faster than a diver off a board. "I didn't mean. I mean…your mother." Her face screwed into a knot, tears bathing her cheeks. "But Will!"

With that, he spun on his heel and strolled inside the factory.

Chapter 13

That night, once Will had tucked Hank into bed after a serious talk about the boy's boundaries, a long walk of his own sounded very good. Parenting was proving tougher than Will had ever thought possible. Had he made the right decision planning to adopt Hank? He might make the boy's life worse with his bad choices. Imagine, not paying attention when the little guy offered to come get him. What kind of father was he? But then again how could it possibly be any worse than it was in Dachau? And he had certainly been wrong about Jeannine.

He might put all the wrong decisions in motion for Hank and have a John Dillinger or a Baby Face Nelson on his hands once Hank grew up. After all the boy had been through, he needed consistency—someone grounded and ever present to be a parent. Someone who understood the ins and outs of what he was doing. That left Will out. Only two years ago he'd been in school, struggling to figure out his own life, let along the life of a small boy.

A groan gurgled from his gut; troubled waters lurked ahead. Will stretched hard to the side, his back giving a telltale crack. Too much stress lately. Lately? For the past two years. He turned the other direction and cracked again. A leisurely walk sounded better and better.

He got only as far as the porch where he slumped into the swing, head down and defeated. No one had really cautioned him about how difficult being a parent would be. Oddly enough, it had been Jeannine who'd warned him in her own sorry way, but she didn't count. She didn't want to be a parent right now, no matter the circumstances. And yet she had brought up a valid point. What did either of them know about being a mother or father? Will might be acting on nothing more solid than emotion, and that could mess Hank up for good. He needed a strong, stable influence to direct his steps. Not a twenty-year-old, wet-behind-the-ears father figure.

A groan escaped his lips while he debated this new phase of his life. There would be school functions, subjects he'd no doubt forgotten. Eventually Hank would ask questions. And Will didn't have the answers. How could he explain to the boy about his parents having been murdered along with hundreds and thousands of others? Hank had nightmares about his experiences. The smell in the camp spoke of death when the soldiers had arrived, probably always had. How much would Hank remember in the coming years? Would he want to talk about it? Would Will know what to say?

Will struggled to control his temper. A tear found its way down his cheek and he wiped it away. No! He'd cried enough when he'd arrived at Dachau. That was the past and he had no intention of giving it one more minute of his thoughts. He was here, now, and he had to make decisions that would affect Hank for the rest of his life. Those choices could not and would not be based on feelings, but rather, sound principles of His Father.

Give me a sign, Lord. I'm sorry I'm asking like a child, but I need to know I made the right decision to bring Hank here.

Lifting his head, he noticed fireflies dotting the yard. He smiled, remembering the nights he'd caught them by the hundreds in Mason jars, thinking he could light his room with them after his parents said lights out. Dozens of fireflies crawling out of the jar in the middle of the night and covering him head to toe had quashed that idea in a hurry. Even as a grown man, bugs didn't particularly appeal to him, but tonight they garnered his attention. *Is this the sign I asked for, Lord?*

His gaze roved the yard until it came to rest on the tree that had held his tire swings. Remnants of the heavy ropes remained where the branch had grown around them—one swing when he was four or five, and another when he'd turned ten. *Tarzan,* that was who he'd imagined himself to be. Flying through the yard on his vines, his feet tucked neatly around the big knot at the end. This had been a happy home. His childhood—a happy childhood. He had been fortunate to have his parents, always encouraging, shaping, nudging him in the right direction.

A worn path had run front to back through the

yard where the boys had taken shortcuts around the house. Not Betty, she'd been too good to misbehave. He laughed, recalling the one time she'd tried hitching her skirt, circling the house. Mother let out a yelp the neighbors must have heard on the other side of town. Never let it be said Mother was openly for independent women, in spite of the fact that she ruled their home with a gentle fist, Dad bowing to her desires as the "general" of the home while he was the "general" at work. He laughed when he remembered all the times Dad would tell the kids, "Go ask your mother. She's the one who makes those decisions."

A rusty bike wheel still decorated the wood shed. Mother said she couldn't bear to part with it. Now he understood. She longed to hang onto the past the best she could. Didn't want to let them grow up, not completely.

He chuckled, reliving the happy times—memories of a contented life, one where his siblings all knew their limitations, but were allowed room to grow and make bad as well as good decisions for themselves.

That was it!

The key to being a good parent meant nothing more than setting boundaries and letting the child discover and learn within those confines. Just as he and Jackson and Betty had. Equal measures of discipline and love—mostly love if he remembered right. If the parent loved enough, the rest didn't matter so much. He could testify to that. While he recalled an occasional dusting of his pants, he mostly remembered the love his parents poured over all three of them. And those moments of discipline were no doubt prompted by love as well.

Good parents. No, wonderful parents, and he wanted to be like them in every way.

He could do this, alone if he had to, but life would be so much better with a wife to share the love with. For the past year, he had supposed that would be Jeannine. How wrong he'd been. But he thanked God he'd realized their differences in time.

The screen door creaked open. Soft footsteps followed.

"Penny for your thoughts."

The voice of an angel interrupted his daydreams. Abby. "You'd need at least a nickel, maybe a dime for all I'm thinking." He smiled up at the shy face hovering above the swing. Abby wrapped her arms around the chain for support and leaned his direction. So beautiful to look at. Even more wonderful to touch. An ache started in his legs and crawled along his spine until the breath, trapped in his throat, longed for an out.

"I might have as much as a quarter. Do I stand here all night guessing or can I sit down? Is it safe?"

By all means. Sit down. Let me wrap you in my arms and hug the air right out of you. "You may, Miss. And what can I do for you?" Because he'd do everything in his power to protect Abby and Hank. He'd been a loyal soldier and expected to be as loyal a man. *No one* had better ever harm his loved ones.

Abby crooked a grin at him, melting what was left of his heart. "You appeared so deep in thought. I'm almost afraid to intrude." She slid into the swing despite her words to the contrary. "I'll take a chance."

"You could never be an intrusion." He patted the

seat closer to where he sat, but Abby kept a respectable distance. One her mother would no doubt be proud of.

"So what troubles you? Are things at work weighing heavily on your mind? Must be different since you came back. Or are you worried about Hank?"

If he hadn't been worried before, he was now. How quickly the little guy had left the yard, all because he wanted to be with Will. Never again would Will take for granted what the boy was telling him. "What else? After today I realized how you can't let your guard down as a parent. Can't take anything for granted. Honestly? I was questioning my ability to be a good father."

Abby reached for his hand. "You are wonderful with him. You're also twenty years old and an overnight parent. Give yourself time to adjust, learn the whys and wherefores. You'll do fine." She sat a bit straighter.

"You're only nineteen. And you seem to do everything right."

"You know, girls have the advantage. There's always someone looking for a sitter when a girl is growing up. I would imagine not a lot of you boys are asked to babysit. I started when I was ten. So you see, we start out in life being trained to do what we do best—be mothers."

He pulled her hands to his mouth and grazed them with his lips. She shivered at his touch. Not wanting to let go, he eyed her, smiling around their fingers. "I could use help, you know. Now that I've committed to raising Hank, I'm going to need all the help I can get." Was he being direct enough? If she didn't get the message, he wasn't sure he could blurt out all he wanted to say. He longed for her to stay, be part of his life. They would raise their children with his brother and her sister. And

Bets and Teddy's kids. He pictured a house full of cousins and brothers and sisters for Hank; knowing Abby, they would all be treated exactly the same.

Abby bit the edge of her lip, a habit he was quickly falling in love with, and pulled her hand back. "Your parents as well as your brother and sister will be there for you. You shouldn't worry so much. They've been wonderful thus far." Then her hands clenched at her sides. "That isn't going to change. Since you returned, a lot of strange things have happened. Give yourself time to adjust, Will. You'll see. Hank is the luckiest little boy in the world."

What I should do is just come out and tell you how I feel. I wish I knew exactly how you feel about me.

He had to take the chance. If he didn't speak up, he might lose her. She could pack up her things and head back to Indiana without so much as a word. The day of the picnic she had warmed to him when he kissed her. "Abby." He cleared his throat for the tenth time since she'd sat down. "I was wondering."

"Yes?" Her eyes lit up, just a bit. Didn't they? Like the fireflies in the yard. Too dark to be sure; he had to trust his judgment. He would tell her how he felt. Lay his emotions out, raw and vulnerable. He had at least a fifty-fifty chance. The most she could do was say no.

He cleared his throat. "Hank is going to need a father *and* a mother. Not just a father."

"One day there will be a Mrs. Judge." She laughed. "Another Mrs. Judge. You'll find a wonderful girl and when you do, she'll love you and Hank both. It would take a heart of stone to turn him away. I can't imagine any woman not loving that precious little boy."

Will inched closer. "Do you love him, Abby?"

Her laughter fell like warm summer rain, straight from heaven to quench his thirst. "You even have to ask? He's so happy over the simplest things. Laughs at a moment's notice. Of course I do, and the girl you fall in love with will, too. I know she will."

He shifted closer to her, sending warmth coursing through him. She didn't pull back. "She who, Abby?"

Heat whipped across Abby's face. Glad he couldn't make out her pink cheeks on the dimly lit porch, she gulped back air. If Will edged any closer, they would have to announce an engagement. It wasn't so dark that she couldn't see his smile—or was that a smirk? He seemed to know without a doubt what he did to her rational thinking, practically throwing her good intentions out the window. He implied a great deal in his speech, but did he really mean what she thought? She loved Hank, that was true, but you couldn't base a lifetime on the love you shared with a child; there had to be more. Will had to love *her* as well, not merely be concerned with getting a mother for his boy. And Abby had never grasped exactly where she stood with him. Was she Hank's babysitter? Barbara's sister? Aunt Abby? His girl? Her face flushed one more time and she had to look away.

He was so near there wasn't room for a firefly between them. "Abigail, who did you mean when you said *she* will love him?" He encircled her hands with his, smothering them in his grasp this time, but his eyes bore down on her face.

"I—uh. Well, I assume you will meet someone now

that you're home. You Judge boys are pretty popular men in town. You're acquainted with everybody here. There must have been plenty of girls in school." She pictured the girls lining up at games waiting for a look from either of the boys.

That smirk—again. "Oh, plenty. They knocked on the door all times of the night and day, waiting to be let in, one by one, my mother and father appalled by each new conquest. I was the ongoing rumor in the town. One scandal here, another scandal there. William Judge, New Hope heartthrob. I guess the newspapers all the way to Chattanooga had their information correct. That's no doubt why Dad supported my decision to go into the army. Got me out of town so all the gossip could die down. Never let it be said William Judge brought shame to his family."

Abby giggled, picturing Will as a rogue. With his good looks and the body of a warrior, she didn't doubt for one second he could be if he wanted to. But she also knew they'd been raised right. "Of course not. We couldn't have Will Judge in a scandal, could we? Oh, Will. You know what I mean. You won't have any trouble finding a lovely woman who will care about Hank. And love you." If she dared, she'd wrap her arms around his neck and kiss him senseless, but he'd think she was a hussy, a girl whose parents had sadly lacked in home training. No, she had to allow him to make the first move, and he didn't seem so inclined. There were days when she wished she could be as forward a girl as Jeannine. How she would love to let all her feelings out.

Will nudged her shoulder. "The truth of the matter is, I've had a thing for a cute girl with pigtails ever since

I kissed her in the hallway five years ago." He tugged a curl of her hair. "She looked up at me with eyes so bright, they lit my heart. I tipped my head and pecked that heart-shaped mouth of hers. Sweet, like honey. So I grabbed her and kissed her again and again until our parents had to step in and drag me away. After a trip to the woodshed with my dad, I learned the error of my ways."

Abby straightened, recognizing that a slightly confused expression crossed her face. Had he kissed her under the mistletoe? No. That was Jackson kissing Barbara. She giggled. He'd heard about that in short order. Abby stopped chuckling and stared at Will's very serious face. "I don't remember that, Will. When did you kiss me?"

A soft groan escaped his lips and his lids drooped. "In my imagination for years. Whenever I closed my eyes and thought about your visit." His stare caused her discomfort. "Each time I took a girl to the movies, she had your face. When I had my first kiss, the girl had pigtails and it was Christmas. No matter what girl I was with, she looked like you. Because that was what I had wanted her to look like. Only I didn't realize she'd grown up. I kept thinking of you as the little Richardson girl I'd fallen for. When I received your last letter, I recall trying to remember how old you were. I didn't ever think of you as an adult. And then Jeannine came along, and she was definitely grown up and without pigtails. I got stars in my eyes." He sighed. "My mistake." He took her all in. His fingers tickled the hair on her neck. "It was pretty clear you didn't like me one bit back then, but I couldn't have been more wrong about you turning into a woman. I should have thought things out better before writing you off as a kid. I should have waited and not fallen for the first pretty face who came along. Because none could compare to you and those freckles. Even today."

A loud whooshing in her ears told her that her heart reacted to his words even if she didn't. "Are you teasing me? I thought you only loved the peanuts back then. Food was the love of *your* life, Will Judge, not me."

"You thought that?" A smile fanned out from his mouth to include his eyes. She loved how brilliant they were, like thousands of stars. "Then you weren't as smart as I gave you credit for. Not at all."

"Oh, men surely don't have any idea what women think, do they? Here I had the worst crush on you, Will. Did you think I was only writing you in the army as a pen pal?"

"As a matter of fact, I did. I thought the reason was because you're Barbara's sister. I had no idea how you felt, and like I said, you were still a kid in my mind." He sat straighter, muscles tensing with each move. "If I recall, in the beginning, when you returned to Indiana, you even said you were writing as my pen pal. And you signed the letters like a pal. Always, Abby. If you'd been interested, why not...Yours Always, Abby?"

"We started writing nearly five years ago when we were kids. I didn't want to appear forward. I didn't even know what forward meant. Mom would have tanned my backside for signing it like that. I guess I've changed since then."

He stared at the stars, and Abby was unsure what more to say without sounding like a fool. Will turned and ran his finger over the freckles on her nose. "You've changed a lot of ways since then."

Abby did her best to stay calm. "My writing to you had nothing to do with Barbara or Jackson."

"Then why did you write me if it wasn't because of your sister?"

"Are you that thick-headed? I liked you. From that first day on the porch." Her face warmed. "I liked you a lot." It seemed she might sit here all night, and he wouldn't take the bait, as Dad would say. Men certainly were dense.

"Now what? Did I say something else wrong?"

"Will Judge, if you don't stop all this nonsense and kiss me, I think I'll have to go home to Indiana and find a boy who—"

His mouth crushed the words from her lips, not stopping even as he murmured, "A boy who what, Abigail Richardson? A boy who'll love you the way you deserve to be loved? Who will honor you as the treasured woman you are? Who will see in you all the qualities he ever longed for in a woman?" His sweet breath tickled her lips. "You are what life is all about, Abby. You're beautiful outside, but you're even more beautiful inside. I've ached to kiss you for so long. Jeannine was nothing but a poor substitute for the kind of woman I've wanted my entire life."

"Will?" She held her breath, hoping.

"Yes?"

Abby wrapped her arms firmly around his neck and snuggled closer. "You talk way too much."

Chapter 14

Did others in the family notice? Abby felt her cheeks for any sign she was blushing…again. Seemed like for the past week all she and Will had done was discuss the future. Without words, it was understood they planned to be together, all three of them. As a family. Her gaze settled on Hank.

He reached out, patted her face and dropped to the side of the bed to say his prayers. Her heart stretched wide to receive all the joy she felt. Like a huge bucket at a well. Each time it appeared to fill up, the bucket got bigger and she was able to hold more water than she could have imagined. She smiled at the silly thought. Is that what love did to someone; made them think, talk, act silly?

Will reached over and squeezed her hand.

"Okay, buddy. Time for bed." He ruffled Hank's hair and tucked the boy in.

They listened outside the door a few minutes before she and Will walked to their favorite place—the porch swing, where they tossed around how they would handle Hank's transition to a more normal life. If possible.

"Do you think he should start school right away or wait an extra year so he can adjust more easily?" Babysitting hadn't prepared her for challenging questions like these. The parents had made the rules; she had merely carried them out.

Will kissed the end of her nose. "Whatever you deem the best. I trust your judgment, Abby. Once we're married, he'll be your son as well as mine, don't forget. And you're a natural with him."

He had more confidence in her than she did. Maybe she'd ask for some advice from Barbara or her mother. All things in good time. "Then, it's settled. We wait a year. Give him a chance to adjust to our marriage."

"All right."

No sense putting off the inevitable, right? Waiting might let him slip through the cracks. They needed to grab that old bull by his worn out horns and move forward. Get Hank involved. "No. Maybe he *should* go to school right away, make friends, have the chance to learn more English." She twisted in Will's grasp and looked up. "Now I'm more confused than ever."

"Abby."

"Yes?"

He clipped the end of her nose and chuckled. "You're making me dizzy with all this talk. We have time. We'll decide about school later. He's only four. And even if he doesn't start until he's six, he's very bright and will do well. I can feel it. Right now let's just concentrate on us.

We have so many plans to make. For us. If we're happy and content he'll be happy and content. I'm sure of it." He laughed out loud and Abby put a finger to his lips.

"Stop. People will think you're crazy."

"I am. Crazy about you. But it just occurred to me. I have to find a house. We can't very well live with my parents." He leaned closer, his grin all telling. "I don't think I'd like the lack of privacy very much."

Abby's face warmed. "No?" How she longed for time alone with Will. Time without the rest of the family. Though she wasn't particularly selfish by nature, she knew without a doubt she would be wanting a great many evenings with no one else but Will at her side. "You'd want me all to yourself?"

"Absolutely." He crushed her in his strong arms. "So I'd better start looking."

"For what?"

"A home. What interests you? There's a lot I don't know about you, and I want to discover every single thing there is."

Abby curled closer. "I'd live in the woodshed with you, Will, but I suppose that wouldn't be the best place for Hank." She sobered. "Do you think he'll get over the nightmares? I can't stay in your room with him forever."

"Sure you can. But, yes. I think he'll get over the nightmares. Once he's convinced we're here and won't ever leave him."

Her hands wrapped around his waist and she leaned her head against his chest, listening to the steady rhythm of his heart. "He has to be able to trust that we'll always be here for him." Her breath rushed between words. "We will make him happy, Will." Abby pulled away, shook her head. Her eyes locked onto his. "That's silly. He's happy right now. You can see it on his face. He trusts us. Loves us. That's all that really matters, right?" Love covered a great many deficits, and they would strive to be good parents. Starting by loving each other, that love would reach all those around them. Wasn't that key to sound relationships? First, you had to love yourself, then have a strong marriage based on mutual love and respect, and then you could add children to the mix. Only they would have a ready-made family.

"I love you, Abby. More than anyone in the entire world."

She burrowed back into his embrace. "I love you, too. And my plan is to make you the happiest man in the world."

She raised her face to his and kissed him. Unable to mask her joy, she smiled and pressed her lips to his again. Why waste time being shy?

"Well, I'd say you're off to a good start."

"I think we'd better go in."

"You do, huh? Well, future Mrs. Judge, I couldn't agree more. Don't like it, but I have to agree it is the sensible thing to do."

"Right. I think it's time for bed."

Will threw his head back and laughed out loud; Abby blushed until she was certain the roots of her hair had turned red. "I meant—"

"No need to be embarrassed. It's just me. And I know what you meant. Abby, you are a pip. That's what Grand used to say. And you're a real pip, Abigail Richardson. I love you so much I can hardly breathe right at the moment."

A noise out front startled them back to reality. Will stood, walked to the edge of the porch and shouted "Who goes there?"

A bicycle with a female rider sat on the walk. "Hi, Will. Abby. I thought I'd drop by and see how Hank's doing. Make sure the little adventurer hasn't gone astray again."

Abby stepped forward, intertwining her arm with Will's, reminding him gently not to say something unkind. "About Hank."

Jeannine's eyes narrowed as she focused on Abby in the fading light. "Yes?"

"I wanted to thank you for finding him when he wandered off. Getting him ice cream was kind of you. Thank you, Jeannine."

The look of astonishment on Jeannine's face vanished in seconds. Instead a sudden smile and out-of-character honey in her words posed a silent threat to Abby. "Why, I'd do anything to help the little fellow. To help Will. Wouldn't I, Will? I'd do what's best for both of you, right?"

Will's fingers dug into the back of Abby's hand. "What do you really want, Jeannine?"

She tossed her hair over her shoulder and chuckled. "Why, William Judge, what are you implying? I'd move heaven and earth for you and Hank. I couldn't help overhearing when I rode up. Making big plans, I see. My, but you are a changeable fellow. One minute in love with me, just days later professing your love for a woman who can't seem to keep track of your little boy. And who stays in *your* room?"

Abby felt her skin turn to ice. Had Jeannine heard

their conversation? The entire conversation? It seemed so. Not that they had said anything wrong, but what would Jeannine make of their plans? Abby realized she must be shocked at the way Will had moved on after their breakup, hadn't stuck around long enough to be sad. She supposed no woman wanted to be replaced so easily. But Jeannine's cruel comments hit the mark.

Will turned to Abby. "I think it's time we went in."

Abby's insides simmered, but she refused to play into this or allow fear to guide her.

"Yes, I think you mentioned something about heading for bed when I rode up." Jeannine waggled her fingers good-bye. "Nightie night, all."

She grasped the handles of the bicycle and steered it toward the road. "Be seeing you around."

Chapter 15

The next morning after breakfast, considering Jeannine's remarks the night before, Will figured he needed to discreetly remind Hank about not leaving the house with anyone outside the family. There could be no more instances where Jeannine might use Hank to get back at him. After all she heard last night, would she try to make trouble for the three of them again?

Will choked on the thought. He could lose Hank! His arm squeezed the little fella's shoulder. "Hank, can I ask you something, son?"

"I son?"

"Sure, buddy."

"I son, I Hank and I buddy. Right?"

"Right, buddy."

"Riggghhht, buddy."

Will sat Hank on his knee, nodded to Mother Judge and indicated a glass of milk with a swigging motion of his hand. "Hank, do you remember your mama and papa?"

"I think so. I have hugs and kisses, but soldiers take hugs and kisses away. Was hugs and kisses Mama and Papa?"

"Maybe." He ruffled the boy's head. "Who took care of you after the hugs and kisses went away, Hank?"

"Soldier lady have yellow hair give me bread."

"A soldier lady?"

"Yup. A *big* soldier lady. When mean boys take my food, she give me bread…sometimes. Why, Will?"

Will's mother put a glass of milk and a cookie within Hank's reach.

"Oh, I just want to be sure we take good care of you. I'm sorry about your mama and papa, buddy. I'll bet they loved you very much."

"Like Miss Jeannine and Miss Abby?"

"Hank, I'd rather you not go with Miss Jeannine anymore."

"She nice, Will. She take me for ice cream and we tell secrets."

Will's stomach lurched. Secrets? "What secrets?"

Hank's fingers fidgeted in his lap. "She come to house and take me for ice cream, tell me it a secret. Say, 'will you keep secret?'"

"What did you tell her?"

"I say yes. I keep secret. She say 'promise?'"

"Did you promise?"

"Sure."

Will groaned and Hank frowned. Will wished Hank had told him this before, and now he had to nip this in the bud. He couldn't have people manipulating Hank when the boy didn't understand the consequences.

"Will?"

"Yes, son?"

"What a secret?"

Will leaned his head back and howled with laughter. As soon as he had the chance, he'd make sure Jeannine understood her place. Would she seriously try and make trouble? Though he'd heard the expression about a woman scorned, he didn't believe she could be that cruel and vindictive. Now after what Hank had told him, he wondered. Anyone with half a brain could see he and Abby were crazy in love. Would her jealousy of Abby be enough to cause Jeannine to take her anger out on all of them? Or was there something else going on with Jeannine?

He tucked Hank under his arm and soothed the furrowed forehead. "Buddy, we need to have a talk about secrets."

"Okay, buddy!"

As usual, Hank listened to every word. At times, with a serious expression, and then suddenly with the innocence that belied his life experiences.

Convinced he'd explained things sufficiently, Will kissed Hank's head. "Time to go get ready for Aunt Barbara, little man. Scoot."

He swatted the seat of Hank's pants, Hank giggling all the way out the door. "Secrets, secrets, secrets."

Judge Miller had scheduled a hearing to determine whether Will would be considered a fit parent for Hank. The hearing was today. Miller told Will that the circuit judge said as long as Will lived in his parents' home until he married one day, they might make an exception, allowing Will's parents to be guardians until then. But they had to go through the process of allowing folks to speak on his behalf, or against him if the situation arose.

Will grabbed his cup of coffee.

The swig of brew burned all the way down his throat. "Mom? What if the court comes up with a reason I can't adopt Hank?"

His mother busied herself at the sink, didn't even turn around.

"Best to put your coat on, son. All the worry won't make a difference, now will it?"

Fingers tensing, Will drummed the counter. "Not worry? Mother, that's easier said than done." He took another sip and poured the rest of the coffee into the sink. "I'll go check on Hank. He's anxious for Aunt Barbara and Grace to come play with him while we're gone, but if he has his way, he'll still be in his dirty overalls."

What if?

It wasn't likely that anyone would say anything bad about him; everyone in town knew and respected him as well as his entire family. At least he thought so. Will hadn't been in any serious trouble in his life.

Well, there was that one time when he and Zak Peters had disassembled the principal's car after school had started, moved it to the roof, and reassembled it there, next to the lightning rod. He could hear Mr. Dunston to this day. The intercommunication system had burped awake during history class.

"Would William Judge...crackle, snap, crackle...and

Zachary Peters report to the principal's office? Right now! And plan to stay after school, fellas, until the car is back in the lot." His father hadn't found it nearly as funny as he and Zak had. But he had to give principal Dunston credit, the man didn't hold a grudge.

Still, his heart raced at the thought he had to prove himself—again. After all, he'd just returned from serving overseas. How much proving of good citizenship did he have to do?

Dragging his feet, he trudged out of the kitchen. He'd better get a move on or he'd be late.

Abby passed him on the stairs. "You all right?"

"Fine." But he wasn't fine. Something at the back of his mind was worrying him. The way Jeannine had looked at them on the porch, as if conveying a message with her own special brand of meanness. But what could she possibly say against him? He hadn't done anything wrong. And why would she say anything anyway? Well, his mother was right, worrying wouldn't help. He needed to get a move on.

Abby reached up and patted his cheek, then pecked his lips. Any other time that would have been an invitation to take her in his arms. "We'll meet you there as soon as Barbara arrives. Jackson said he'd drive us over, so you scoot." No holding her today. Not now. Right at the moment the only thing that mattered was getting to the courthouse and finalizing his right to make Hank legally his own little boy.

He ran a thumb over her jaw. "I love you, Abby. I'm not sure how I lived before. Without you, I mean."

Her smile breathed new life into his determination.

* * *

When he jumped out of the Studey, he stared at the old stone building that served as the local courthouse, jail, police department and barbershop. As nervous as he felt, he couldn't stifle a chuckle. The barber pole in the front attested to the fact the town needed all the revenue it could get. Why else would they rent out the miniscule space in the corner to the barber?

Barber pole one side, police sign on the other and the distinguished courthouse in the middle. He loved this town. And everything about it. Having lived here all his life, he knew people respected him. A rush of relieved air blew through his lips. Why had he been so worried? This town's people cared about each and every member, and no one would want to stand in the way of his adopting Hank. If anything, he expected a band of folks to show up for support.

When he entered the courthouse, his steps faltered. He might have to change that assessment. Jeannine waited inside wearing a dark suit, her legs crossed at the ankles. Miss Prim and Proper.

She sat on a granite bench and patted the seat next to her as he turned the corner. Her face, with a smile that defied credibility, lit up the minute he entered. "Over here, Will. Where's your family?"

"They're coming. Had to wait for Barbara to babysit Hank." Not that it was any of her business. He couldn't imagine why she was here. Hopefully just a parking ticket and nothing to do with him.

"Oh, dear. He's not coming? I so looked forward to seeing him again."

His brow rose. Of course she did, about as much as

she looked forward to a tooth extraction. Now what was her game? He should probably try to find out before going into the court. He took a seat as far on the other end of the bench as he could get.

No sense beating about the bush. Only wastes time, as his dad would say. "What are you doing here, Jeannine?"

At first she ignored his question, instead twisting a hankie in her fingers. Then with a sad expression said, "Oh, just stopped by to see if you've come to your senses and had a change of heart."

He suddenly felt as rigid as the stone bench beneath him. Immoveable. Inflexible. If he opened his mouth, he would say something horrific, so he studied the portraits on the walls. Presidents, local politicians. "Jeannine. There's no change of heart. Our beliefs are different, our hopes, our dreams. We would have made each other miserable. I've moved on. You should, too."

She flipped the handkerchief against her skirt and pouted, a posture he had learned suited her fine and him not at all. "Oh, you moved on, all right. Did you even wait five minutes? You couldn't have loved me very much, not like you claimed to in your letters. And how do you know you love her if you're so inconstant? You might change your mind again."

"Jeannine. Enough!" Will's hand tightened until his fingers dug into his thigh.

She dabbed at a tearless eye.

"Jeannine, my whole world right now is Hank and what's best for him."

She slid closer. "Mom and I were talking about this very thing the other day. She said we'd be more than—"

He brushed her hand away. *Oh, Lord. Don't allow me to say things I'll regret.* "Stop, now. There is no *we* anymore. There's you and there's me. And if we're to be absolutely honest with each other, I was lonely and you wanted someone to write to. A combination for disaster. I'm not sure how we ever allowed ourselves to turn to talk of marriage. We didn't know each other very well. I'm very sorry if I've hurt you. That was never my intention."

She backed away from him and sat against the wall, her arms across her chest, her face a mishmash of anger, disgust and something else. Something almost vengeful. "We hardly had a chance at all. That Miss-What's-Her-Name kept sticking her nose in. Why is she in New Hope anyway?"

Because God is kinder to me than I deserve. He glanced up as her eyes sparked outrage.

"Well? Why *is* she here?"

"She came here to help her sister." He lowered his voice so they wouldn't attract attention.

"Then she should stay at her sister's house more often. I know how girls like that are, Will."

"I'm sure you do, Jeannine, but Abby's not like that. We've known each other a long time."

She leveled a glare at him. Will slid to the other side of the bench, then stood. "I would never hurt you on purpose, but we're different people than we thought we were in our letters. I wish you all the best. Truly, I do."

Jeannine rose, brushed imaginary lint from her skirt and walked in the direction of the courtroom. She stopped a few steps outside the door and smirked over her shoulder. "Being jilted is very embarrassing, Will."

"Jilted? Calling off an engagement is not the same as jilting someone!"

"Really? That's not how it feels to me." She opened the door and strode into the courtroom.

Chapter 16

Will's family entered the courthouse in a rush of noise and a warm breeze. "Hey, about time you arrived. I thought you'd deserted me for good. Ashamed to be seen with me, huh?"

A hug from his folks followed. Abby stayed back, away from inquiring eyes.

Will strode to her side and grabbed her hand. "Okay, this is it. Walk me to the guillotine. Off with their heads!" He leaned in and whispered, "And you're the queen of my heart. So protect me when they say all sorts of horrible things." He winked, hoping this meeting would be quick and easy, not frightening.

During the hearing Dr. Zachman, who'd brought Will into the world, Mrs. Schroeder, his aunt's German neighbor, the sheriff and a dozen other citizens of New Hope offered glowing reports of Will's good, sound character going all the way back to his childhood. The recitations had become downright embarrassing.

Will finished the meeting by laying out his immediate and future plans for the boy. "So you see, Your Honor, I've already been in contact with the school to glean some advice from a few of my former teachers about the best way to get Henryk ready for an American school."

Judge Miller peered over his reading glasses; he looked over Will's shoulder to his parents and back to Will again. "Young man, the court recognizes what you did for this boy."

Will didn't want accolades. He'd only done what anyone would have. "He did more for me, Your Honor. He saved my life."

The judge slapped his palm on the desk. "Don't interrupt me, young fella. Now, as I was saying. We have to take all matters into account. Where will the boy thrive the most? Where can he feel safe, secure? Who will provide a stable and lasting home, not just a temporary stopping-off point?" His face softened. "We all want to believe we will do the right things when we're presented with opportunities. But very often life itself gets in the way of our good intentions. Now, you're a young man, your future still being determined. I understand you and this pretty little gal are planning to get married. Where will that leave the boy? Where will the little fellow fit in then?" He raised his hand to stop Will from talking. "Just a rhetorical question, William. But these are the kinds of situations I have to consider before rendering a decision. We will take a break for lunch and then come back. I'll have my decision by then."

* * *

Abby watched the disappointment spread over Will's face. Was it possible the judge would decide to keep Hank from Will? Perhaps Barbara and Jackson would step in. Of course they would. Or Mr. and Mrs. Judge might adopt Hank.

Will edged close and took her by the elbow. "Shall we go?"

Abby did her best to smile. "Your mother and I have sandwiches at home."

Will's eyes held more sadness than she'd seen in a very long time. "I'm not hungry, if truth be told. If Judge Miller doesn't allow me to adopt Hank, I'm not sure I'll ever be hungry again."

Abby patted his sleeve. "This will all work out. Have faith, Will. The same kind of faith that kept your mother going when they told her you were missing is the same faith that will do right by Hank. You didn't waver all that time overseas. Don't waver now."

His lips broke into a smile, but it didn't fan over his face, to his eyes, where Will's smiles truly resided. "I do have faith, Abby, it's just… What if God doesn't think I'd be the best person for Hank? If I truly believe in God's will, then I have to accept it if God doesn't want me to be the person to raise him. I'm not sure I can step out of his life at this point."

"You can really say that? Do you think He allowed Hank to be the first prisoner you came in contact with and then to save your life only to snatch him from you? Will, I'm disappointed in you."

"What?"

She grinned. "You know better. God isn't like that.

He doesn't get our hopes up when we know we are on the side of right only to dash them against a rock. Hank will become your son. I have no doubt whatsoever. He couldn't have a better father than you." She tugged at his arm. "Now, let's go home and have a sandwich so you'll have the strength to chase your little boy around the rest of the day."

Again the forced smile. Abby didn't doubt Will's beliefs for one second, but like everyone else, that faith was tested from time to time. And often, God would show himself in the strangest ways if only folks kept their eyes open.

Abby pushed Will toward the door, but couldn't help noticing that Jeannine was striding toward Judge Miller.

After lunch when they all returned to the courtroom, Judge Miller's face had turned into a dark cloud. He cleared his throat while everyone took their seats. Will swallowed hard over a huge lump in his throat. What had happened?

"Some issues have come to light and I feel I must address them," the judge began.

Will glanced over at Jeannine. She sat upright, her eyes straight ahead, but he caught the slightest smirk on her face.

"William, I see no way around this. I must ask some difficult questions." He cleared his throat and sounded like a bullfrog. "It has been brought to my attention that you were recently engaged to one young woman and now you are engaged to another. In addition, a certain young lady might be sharing your room. Now, I'm not generally one to listen to gossip, but the boy's care is in my hands. I need to know exactly what is going on."

There were stirrings and whispers in the courtroom. At all of the commotion, Abby's eyes filled with tears. Will longed to comfort her, but one look from him, and she ran from the room.

Will wanted to follow her, but knew he had to stay and see this through. He spoke up. "Sir, I have no desire to ruin a woman's reputation. I don't know exactly what you've been told, but I'm guessing there is barely enough truth to keep *someone* in this courtroom from perjuring herself."

"That's a serious accusation, young man."

Will's mother rose from her seat. She walked gingerly to Jeannine's side and forced the girl to her feet. "Missy, I do believe we need to talk with Judge Miller." With a gasp, Jeannine struggled, but his mother won out and she marched Jeannine to the front of the room. Everyone present could hear as Judge Miller got an earful about the standards upheld in the Judge home and what actually had happened with respect to Abby's staying with Hank in Will's room.

The judge peered at Jeannine over his glasses. "Is that the correct version, Miss? And think before you answer, because if Mrs. Judge is correct about your lying to this court, the penalty to you will be severe."

"Well, sir, I—I, uh. Well, you see, I heard them talking and I thought… I only told you what I thought I heard them say. And after all, until she came along I was engaged to Will Judge…you see."

Judge Miller slapped his hand on the desk and glared

at her. "I certainly do see. You may go back to your seat. But don't leave this courtroom until I tell you to."

Will's mother walked Jeannine back to her seat and all present could hear her comments. "Young lady, your mother would be appalled to know what you've been saying. She's a good, God-fearing woman, and furthermore, she'd be disgusted at what you've been doing. I've heard about all those soldiers' letters."

Jeannine paled as she took her seat. She seemed to shrivel against the back of the bench like a dirigible with no hot air.

Will's mother took her seat, her lips pursed.

The judge raised a brow. "William Judge, approach the bench."

When Will was standing before him he said, "I think most of my questions have been answered. Now, son, I can understand how a man could get engaged to the wrong woman when he's far from home and fighting in a war. And it takes guts to admit you're wrong and break off an engagement. I also understand that you and Miss Richardson have known each other for some years, and according to your mother's testimony, she is a fine young woman. But right now you're a single man and I think it's best that a child have the stability of a home with both father and mother if at all possible. So here's what we're going to do. The court will allow Mayor and Mrs. Charles Judge to be guardians to Henryk Drobinski until you marry. At that time we'll revisit this decision." He slammed the gavel and winked at Will.

"But Your Honor."

"Not another word, young fella." He sniffed and his gaze narrowed on Will. He leaned down and whispered in Will's ear, "Just a suggestion, but I'd try flowers if I were you. And if they work, I want an invitation to the wedding."

As he shook Will's hand, his eyes focused over Will's shoulder. Will turned to observe Jeannine crouching down in her seat. A sour expression overtook Judge Miller's face. "And now to you, young lady." Will almost felt sorry for Jeannine.

Life didn't always go as planned; sometimes life, like baseball at recess, threw curves. Abby would have smiled if she hadn't been so miserable, remembering how in fifth grade she had worn shorts under her dresses at school so she could slide the bases like a boy. Explaining scrapes and bruises had become an everyday chore for her, but her love of all things boy couldn't be disciplined or shamed out of her. And for good reason; her father heartily approved of girls playing outside, rough and tumbling for good health and happiness.

Well, so much for a healthy, happy life. Now she'd been branded worse than Hester Prynne. And she hadn't done anything wrong! All because of a woman scorned.

Abby's hands slapped the arms of the chair and she rose to her feet. No sense whining. After the shame in the courtroom, Will could lose custody of Hank. And how could she hold her head up in this town when her reputation had been called into question? Would anyone believe the truth? She should simply go home and forget everything that had happened.

A sound like geese honking crept through the partially open windows. Abby strained to listen. She lifted the bedroom window to the top to find the source of all the noise. Car horns? And shouting? Then she saw the vehicles lining the road—a steady stream of cars and trucks nearly filled the dirt road Barbara and Jackson lived on. And in the front drove Will like a commander of his troops. He hopped from the car and sprinted for Hank who was playing with his truck in the front yard.

What on earth?

Forgetting her humiliation momentarily, Abby dashed down the stairs and opened the door.

The two men in her life sprinted to the steps and met her on the porch. Will set Hank in the swing, took Abby in his arms and kissed the tears from her cheeks. "No one believed her, Abby. No one. My mother set the record straight. And she didn't do it very tactfully. The judge awarded temporary custody to my folks until we get married."

She pulled back and stared. "What are you talking about, Will?"

"I found out I wasn't the only guy Jeannine had been writing to overseas."

"What?"

"My mother is part of the Women's Auxiliary. They talk—a lot. Actually, it's how Mother knew about Jeannine. I wondered why she and Father acted so peculiar at the train station. She'd heard things—not-so-nice things. According to Hannah someone-or-something, Jeannine's plan was to wait at home for the first Yank who came back so she could marry him. End of story."

"No. The girl must have heard wrong, Will. No woman would do that." She swallowed hard, forcing the doubt away. "Are you sure?"

"You're here for a reason, Abby." His words spoke to her heart.

"I don't know, Will. I seemed to have caused you only trouble." But as her eyes refilled, her gaze rested on his mouth. He wasn't angry about what had happened in the courthouse? Had God put her here for a reason? "What reason is that?"

"You've helped a grown man learn to live life the way it should be lived and a little boy to feel loved and secure. You've brought laughter into our lives. Joy into the family. And I don't know what I'd do without you." His arms tightened. "I'd like to ask you something very important."

Then he dropped to one knee and reached into his pocket while Hank giggled and clapped. "Ask 'er, ask 'er, Will," he cried.

Abby felt the color drain from her face. "Ask me what, Will?"

"Abigail, you taught me what true love was, every day, in every way. And to keep the faith when all else was failing me. I don't want to live without you. I can't live without you. If you left, a huge part of me would go, forever. We've known each other for years. I was simply too foolish to accept you as a grown woman. I know better now. Please, let's make it official by setting the date. Let's not assume anything. Say you'll marry me."

He slipped a beautiful diamond ring on her finger, and Abby gasped.

Hank jumped out of the swing and dashed to Will's side. He prodded Will with his finger. "Say kocham cie, and hold yer arms out. Like this. Tell 'er, Will. Tell 'er you loves her this much." His arms opened wide.

Will winked at Hank and smiled. "Like this?" His arms opened wide and he hugged Hank. "Kocham cie, Hank." He stood to his feet, Hank next to his side, nodding furiously. "Kocham cie, Abby. I *loves* you this much." His arms spread wide again. Not waiting for her to answer, he drew her into his grasp.

When the air whooshed from her chest, she giggled like a kid.

"Please say you'll marry me while the flowers are still blooming. I want the same love Barbara and Jack have. The same love Bets and Teddy have. The gazebo we built for Betty's wedding seems to be the marriage maker."

Abby buried her head in his chest. "No, ours was a love made in heaven. God brought me here at a time when I needed to get my priorities straightened out. And it worked. I love you, Will. All those letters you thought came from a kid, came from a heart that needed mending. I've loved you since I first saw you munching peanuts on the porch of your parents' house."

He groaned, his warm breath whispering against her cheek. "In spite of that, you mean."

Abby burrowed deeper into his arms. "No, because of it. I love you. And I love Hank." She reached over and ruffled the hair on Hank's head then looked deep into Will's eyes. With a hitch in her words, she said "Of course, I'll make it official. I'll marry you. There isn't a man alive I'd rather spend the rest of my life with." She pretended to scribble on a pad of paper. "Yours always, Abby."

Will's eyes scoured her face until, at last, his lips lowered to hers. He explored her mouth softly at first, and then in a way that surprised them both. A stirring at their side separated them.

"Yucky," the small voice said.

But it wasn't yucky to Abby. Will's mouth, warm against hers, promised a lifetime of happiness. She smiled at Hank, but returned Will's kiss, drinking in the sweetness of his love. His arms crushed her firmly to him and she didn't have any plans to let go, not even when people began to empty from the cars. A quick glance up and a noisy reunion of folks returned them to their surroundings once again. Abby's face flamed hot. "I think we have more of an audience than just one."

Townspeople hurried to them with all measure of good wishes.

"Congratulations, you two."

"Will, did she say yes?" A hand clapped Will's back and Abby held out her hand for all to see the ring.

"How about a late summer wedding? Give her folks time to get here."

"Oh, Abigail," a woman gushed, "I'm so happy for you two."

An older man shouted from the middle of the pack, "Hey there, Willie boy, when you gonna tie the knot? Way to go, young fella."

"You Judges have swell weddings. Planning already?"

Hank moved the fingers covering his eyes and grinned. "He ask 'er, he did."

Will pecked Abby's lips and lifted his mouth for just a second. "I think we'd better make them happy. They might turn into an angry mob otherwise." He lifted his eyebrows playfully and turned to face the yard. Then he pumped a fist of victory in the air and shouted at the top of his voice. "She said yes!"

Abby peeked from the corner of her eyes, her face hotter than a chili pepper. "Can I at least call my parents first and tell them it's official before the entire town finds out?"

"Honey, I'm afraid it's too late for that."

Chapter 17

Crickets chirped, the sun offered warm, dry days and birds sang unusually loud, as if announcing the upcoming wedding. Will walked through the backyard, imagining all the wedding plans the women had made. He was afraid to ask for details, sure he'd be forced into the decorating.

The gazebo Jackson had built for his sister Betty's wedding would, once again, be pressed into service for the marriage ceremony. And, once again, his mother assured him flowers from her garden would twine around and cover the wooden frame from top to bottom. Abby had told him how much this setting meant to her.

Anxious to start their new life together, Will and Abby had decided then and there not to wait for a spring wedding. Summer was now here and summer it would be. They would not put the wedding off for almost an entire year. The families saw no reason to delay, either.

The quicker they married, the happier they would be, and they could adopt Hank that much sooner as well.

However, Will had laughed at her initial reaction to a wedding in less than a month, but after Barbara and Betty put their heads together with suggestions flying back and forth, Abby had thrown her hands in the air and conceded defeat. Afterward he and his father had laughed at how quickly the three of them arranged every detail. And that's when Will understood Abby didn't want to wait any more than he did.

Mr. and Mrs. Richardson, soon to be his new in-laws, arrived the first week of August, not wanting to be left out. Excited to see them again, Will took the time the very first evening to ask Mr. Richardson officially for his daughter's hand.

"Well, young fella. I know she won't go hungry. I've seen you with enough peanuts to feed an elephant."

Will sensed what Mr. Richardson tried to say, but couldn't: *You'd* better *take care of my little girl or you'll have me to answer to.* And as a father now, Will realized they shared a bond that only fathers understood. *Love me, love my child and be responsible around her.* "Thank you, sir."

"None of that 'sir' stuff. Feel free to call me anything that's nice. Dad, Pa, or Your Honor." He laughed aloud. "Maybe you could just call me Gramps. Seems like I'm a grandpa all over again. Say, but isn't that angel, Gracie, a beauty?" He slapped Will's back. "And Hank is a firecracker. Such a smart little guy. All boy, my new grandson."

The whole Richardson family had welcomed Will

much as they had Jackson when he and Barbara had married.

Even his future sister-in-law, Dorothy, had opened her young heart to him. And to Hank, when at last they met.

"I Hank." He'd pointed at his chest. "Pleased to meet you, Aunt Dot."

Dot had kissed his cheeks over and over while he snuggled closer, but in spite of himself, he still managed to complain, "'Nuff. Okay?"

Will loved that the families spent two wonderful weeks enjoying each other's company, getting to know one another all over again, and Hank managed to work his way into each heart the same way he'd burrowed into Will's.

With one last glimpse at the gazebo, Will went inside to find his girl.

Sunny with a sprinkling of fluffy white clouds in the late August sky, the perfect day arrived at last.

Arms filled with black-eyed susans, daisies and baby's breath, Abby waited at the back door. The look on Will's face let her know their lives would be overflowing with—excitement! The good and the bad. The sad and the happy. But their love promised both of them a full life.

The long walk toward the gazebo sent flutters through Abby's stomach. Will waited in the front, handsome in his black suit, white shirt and dark blue tie. His eyes never off her for even a second. Holding Jackson's hand, Hank wriggled at Will's side, clutching at the tight matching blue tie around his neck, but his smile fit him perfectly.

Once at the end of the petal-strewn walkway, holding Will's hands, Abby wondered if there were anyone else in the entire world because she saw only him. His eyes drank her in. The muscle that pulsed in his jaw when he was under stress danced a jig. And his hands, warm around hers, offered a promise for the future. How long they stood there, she wasn't sure. She vaguely remembered mumbling things, but Will was all that mattered. Her love rose higher and higher with each beat of her heart the same way the pulse in his wrist announced to her fingers he would always love her.

Then, pulling her from her daydream, the minister said, "You may kiss the bride."

Will didn't hesitate a second. He crushed her to him. His lips hovered until she longed to scream the words *kiss me, Will!* And he did. He kissed her, again and again. "And I have no intention of ever letting you go. I hope that's all right." He devoured her with his eyes.

"Of course," she murmured close so only he could hear. "Don't ever let me out of your arms."

Face warm, she looked up, noticing the stares from their guests. She chewed the edge of her lip, knowing her mother hated when she did that. Will leaned closer and returned his own intimate message. "Please hold that thought until we're alone and I promise not to let you out of my arms." He tucked her arm firmly in his grasp.

The return stroll across the walkway accompanied cheers from their guests. With each greeting, Will dropped a kiss on Abby's welcoming lips. She couldn't get enough of him. Her eyes glistened with a tenderness Will's face gladly mirrored. Hank skipped behind them, grinning from ear to ear but covering his face whenever they kissed.

Abby accepted the wishes of her friends and family. Her mother's face beamed, her father's lip trembled ever so slightly. Dorothy clapped her hands, a smile permanently fixed on her face.

Will stopped at the end of the walkway, drew Abby's fingers to his lips and kissed her one more time. "For good luck."

"We don't need luck," Abby said, his affection irresistible. "We have each other. And we have God."

When at last they arrived and formed the receiving line across from tables laden with the light fare of wedding cake, punch, finger sandwiches and other delectable treats, Abby's father joined them. He laughed, clapped Will on the back and said, "Welcome to the family, son. I still have one more daughter left. Do you have any more brothers?"

"No, sir, but there is this friend of ours."

* * * * *

REQUEST YOUR FREE BOOKS!

2 FREE INSPIRATIONAL NOVELS
PLUS 2
FREE
MYSTERY GIFTS

Love Inspired®

LIDIR13R

REQUEST YOUR FREE BOOKS!

2 FREE RIVETING INSPIRATIONAL NOVELS
PLUS 2 FREE MYSTERY GIFTS

YES! Please send me 2 FREE Love Inspired® Suspense novels and my 2 FREE mystery gifts (gifts are worth about $10). After receiving them, if I don't wish to receive any more books, I can return the shipping statement marked "cancel." If I don't cancel, I will receive 4 brand-new novels every month and be billed just $4.74 per book in the U.S. or $5.24 per book in Canada. That's a savings of at least 21% off the cover price. It's quite a bargain! Shipping and handling is just 50¢ per book in the U.S. and 75¢ per book in Canada.* I understand that accepting the 2 free books and gifts places me under no obligation to buy anything. I can always return a shipment and cancel at any time. Even if I never buy another book, the two free books and gifts are mine to keep forever.

123/323 IDN F5AN

Name	(PLEASE PRINT)

Address	Apt. #

City	State/Prov.	Zip/Postal Code

Signature (if under 18, a parent or guardian must sign)

Mail to the Harlequin® Reader Service:
IN U.S.A.: P.O. Box 1867, Buffalo, NY 14240-1867
IN CANADA: P.O. Box 609, Fort Erie, Ontario L2A 5X3

**Are you a current subscriber to Love Inspired Suspense books
and want to receive the larger-print edition?
Call 1-800-873-8635 or visit www.ReaderService.com.**

* Terms and prices subject to change without notice. Prices do not include applicable taxes. Sales tax applicable in N.Y. Canadian residents will be charged applicable taxes. Offer not valid in Quebec. This offer is limited to one order per household. Not valid for current subscribers to Love Inspired Suspense books. All orders subject to credit approval. Credit or debit balances in a customer's account(s) may be offset by any other outstanding balance owed by or to the customer. Please allow 4 to 6 weeks for delivery. Offer available while quantities last.

Your Privacy—The Harlequin® Reader Service is committed to protecting your privacy. Our Privacy Policy is available online at www.ReaderService.com or upon request from the Harlequin Reader Service.
We make a portion of our mailing list available to reputable third parties that offer products we believe may interest you. If you prefer that we not exchange your name with third parties, or if you wish to clarify or modify your communication preferences, please visit us at www.ReaderService.com/consumerschoice or write to us at Harlequin Reader Service Preference Service, P.O. Box 9062, Buffalo, NY 14269. Include your complete name and address.

LISDIR13R

REQUEST YOUR FREE BOOKS!

2 FREE INSPIRATIONAL NOVELS
PLUS 2
FREE
MYSTERY GIFTS

Love Inspired

HISTORICAL
INSPIRATIONAL HISTORICAL ROMANCE

YES! Please send me 2 FREE Love Inspired® Historical novels and my 2 FREE mystery gifts (gifts are worth about $10). After receiving them, if I don't wish to receive any more books, I can return the shipping statement marked "cancel." If I don't cancel, I will receive 4 brand-new novels every month and be billed just $4.74 per book in the U.S. or $5.24 per book in Canada. That's a savings of at least 21% off the cover price. It's quite a bargain! Shipping and handling is just 50¢ per book in the U.S. and 75¢ per book in Canada.* I understand that accepting the 2 free books and gifts places me under no obligation to buy anything. I can always return a shipment and cancel at any time. Even if I never buy another book, the two free books and gifts are mine to keep forever.

102/302 IDN F5CY

Name	(PLEASE PRINT)	
Address		Apt. #
City	State/Prov.	Zip/Postal Code

Signature (if under 18, a parent or guardian must sign)

Mail to the Harlequin® Reader Service:
IN U.S.A.: P.O. Box 1867, Buffalo, NY 14240-1867
IN CANADA: P.O. Box 609, Fort Erie, Ontario L2A 5X3

Want to try two free books from another series?
Call 1-800-873-8635 or visit www.ReaderService.com.

* Terms and prices subject to change without notice. Prices do not include applicable taxes. Sales tax applicable in N.Y. Canadian residents will be charged applicable taxes. Offer not valid in Quebec. This offer is limited to one order per household. Not valid for current subscribers to Love Inspired Historical books. All orders subject to credit approval. Credit or debit balances in a customer's account(s) may be offset by any other outstanding balance owed by or to the customer. Please allow 4 to 6 weeks for delivery. Offer available while quantities last.

Your Privacy—The Harlequin® Reader Service is committed to protecting your privacy. Our Privacy Policy is available online at www.ReaderService.com or upon request from the Harlequin Reader Service.

We make a portion of our mailing list available to reputable third parties that offer products we believe may interest you. If you prefer that we not exchange your name with third parties, or if you wish to clarify or modify your communication preferences, please visit us at www.ReaderService.com/consumerschoice or write to us at Harlequin Reader Service Preference Service, P.O. Box 9062, Buffalo, NY 14269. Include your complete name and address.

ReaderService.com

Manage your account online!

- Review your order history
- Manage your payments
- Update your address

*We've designed
the Harlequin® Reader Service
website just for you.*

Enjoy all the features!

- Reader excerpts from any series
- Respond to mailings and special monthly offers
- Discover new series available to you
- Browse the Bonus Bucks catalog
- Share your feedback

Visit us at:
ReaderService.com

HEARTSONG
PRESENTS

Look out for 4 new
Heartsong Presents books next month!

**Every month 4 inspiring faith-filled
romances will be available in stores.**

These contemporary and historical Christian
romances emphasize God's role in every
relationship and reinforce the importance of
faith, hope and love.